Bello
hidden talent rediscovered

Bello is a digital-only imprint of Pan Macmillan,
established to breathe new life into previously published,
classic books.

At Bello we believe in the timeless power of the imagination,
of a good story, narrative and entertainment, and we want to
use digital technology to ensure that many more readers
can enjoy these books into the future.

We publish in ebook and print-on-demand formats
to bring these wonderful books to new audiences.

www.panmacmillan.com/imprint-publishers/bello

Richmal Crompton

Richmal Crompton (1890–1969) is best known for her thirty-eight books featuring William Brown, which were published between 1922 and 1970. Born in Lancashire, Crompton won a scholarship to Royal Holloway in London, where she trained as a schoolteacher, graduating in 1914, before turning to writing full-time. Alongside the William novels, Crompton wrote forty-one novels for adults, as well as nine collections of short stories.

Richmal Crompton

FELICITY—
STANDS BY

BELL◉

First published in 1950 by George Newnes Limited

This edition published 2017 by Bello
an imprint of Pan Macmillan
20 New Wharf Road, London N1 9RR
Associated companies throughout the world

www.panmacmillan.com/imprint-publishers/bello

ISBN 978-1-5098-5946-7 EPUB
ISBN 978-1-5098-5944-3 HB
ISBN 978-1-5098-5945-0 PB

Typeset by Ellipsis Digital Limited, Glasgow

Visit **www.panmacmillan.com** to read more about all our books
and to buy them. You will also find features, author interviews and
news of any author events, and you can sign up for e-newsletters
so that you're always first to hear about our new releases.

Contents

Chapter   Page

1. Felicity Procures a Secretary   1

2. Three Birds with One Stone   18

3. Felicity and Socialism   39

4. Felicity Joins "The Oranges"   54

5. Fate and Emerson Smith   68

6. Felicity and the Little Blind God   89

7. Felicity Comes to Town   104

8. Felicity and the Poet   118

9. Felicity Makes Amends   134

10. Mrs. Fanning's Psychic Experience   152

11. Mrs. Franklin's Maid   169

12. L'envoi   179

Chapter One

Felicity Procures a Secretary

Norma Felicity Montague Harborough (known to her immediate friends as "Pins," which tradition asserted to have been her earliest attempt at the pronunciation of her own name) leant back in the corner of a third-class railway carriage with a sigh of content. Upon her lips was a smile which would have conveyed only sweetness and innocence to anyone unacquainted with her character. To anyone acquainted with her character it would have conveyed the simple fact that she had successfully brought off some unusually outrageous piece of devilry.

Felicity had the face that goes with a stained-glass window saint of the Middle Ages. She had a complexion of smooth ivory faintly tinged with rose. Her exquisite lips drooped wistfully at the corners except when they quivered in sudden mischief. Her eyes—of vivid, speedwell blue—held an engaging, childlike candour except when they twinkled demurely behind their fringe of black lashes. Her hair—of a rich red-gold—curled softly about her face and fell in a thick plait down her back.

At the end of about half an hour's close observation a very, very careful observer would have come to the conclusion that Felicity was not quite as saintlike as at first sight she looked. Felicity was not. Yet she appreciated to the full and extracted the utmost value from those wistfully drooping lips and clear, candid eyes with which an all-seeing Providence had endowed her.

Felicity had (within the last hour) left school. She had attained the age of sixteen, and a family conclave consisting of Sir Digby Harborough, her grandfather, Lady Montague, her aunt, and John, her elder brother, had decided that her education had now reached the stage when she might leave school and continue her studies quietly at home with suitable instructors until she came out. Felicity quite approved of the decision that she should leave school. With regard to the quiet study at home she had her own ideas.

The journey home from school at the end of the term was generally in the nature of solemn ceremonial. Those youthful scions of the British aristocracy whose education was entrusted to Miss Barlow, of Minter House, Eastbourne (the oldest-established institution of its kind in England, where the scholars are supplied with an extensive knowledge of Culture in all its branches and prepared to take their place in Society with a capital S—vide the prospectus passim), were guarded and treasured with a thoroughness worthy of the time of Victoria the Great and Good. Always one of Miss Barlow's trusted underlings accompanied Felicity to the London terminus and handed her over in person to Lady Montague, that overpoweringly stately and condescending being who was Felicity's aunt.

This term Felicity had represented to Miss Barlow that, having left school, she had no need of the "escort" which the prospectus advertised as being provided for every member of the school on the journey to and from Minter House. Miss Barlow waved Felicity's representation aside with an august and indignant hand. Felicity, nowise daunted, wrote to her aunt to suggest that as she had now left school she should come on home from the London terminus by herself. Felicity's aunt had merely replied that she was surprised and shocked at Felicity's suggestion and that she would go to the London terminus as usual to receive Felicity in person from the hands of the Minter House underling. She added that it had never yet been said that a niece of hers had travelled down from London alone. Felicity, inspired solely by an inborn wilfulness and a desire of issuing a declaration of independence, decided that it was time it should be said.

It was not easy to arrange, but Felicity, when her mind was set on her own purpose, did not grudge time or thought or trouble.

In the typed notice of the time of her arrival that she was given to enclose in her last letter home Felicity deliberately altered the time of the train to a later one.

She arrived with the underling at the London terminus. Fate was on Felicity's side. It was the underling's last term, as it was Felicity's. The underling, who was soon to enter the bonds of holy matrimony, was met at the London terminus by a roseate male. Forthwith, to the underling, Felicity ceased to exist. She received Felicity's demure explanation that "Aunt would be coming a little later and it was all right and please don't wait," almost as in a trance, and after pressing Felicity's hand with her eyes fixed ecstatically on the roseate male's and saying absently that she'd got her ticket, hadn't she, she drifted away clinging ecstatically to the arm of the male, whose roseateness glowed to a glorious vermilion at the touch of the underling's clinging arm.

Felicity was thrilled to find herself upon the London terminus alone, unchaperoned, unescorted, unguarded. It was a delightful experience. The blue eyes danced, the wistful lips quivered. Felicity felt really and truly grown up at last. It was a gorgeous feeling.

She was roused from her dream by a respectful porter with a flowing moustache, who had put her luggage on to a truck and now told her it was time to be going to the train. Felicity didn't want to be bothered with luggage. She scribbled a note on a piece of paper which she found in her bag: "Gone on home by earlier train.—F.," folded it across, wrote "Lady Montague" on the outside, and handed it to the porter, telling him to give it to a tall stout lady in a large black hat and furs (Lady Montague always wore large black hats and furs, whatever the weather or the time of year), who would come later to claim the luggage and demand Felicity.

The delivering of messages to ladies in large black hats and furs was not the porter's work, and to anyone else he would have said so. It was not the half-crown that Felicity gave him from her purse that persuaded him to undertake it. It was the glance that Felicity gave him from her speedwell-blue eyes. Life had already taught Felicity in more crises than one the proper use of speedwell-blue eyes.

3

So, though Miss Barlow had provided Felicity with a first-class ticket, Felicity, singing to herself and treading on air, free, unchaperoned, having left school, with all the world before her, and the delicious sensation of defiant lawlessness that her escapade had given her, leapt lightly into a third-class carriage. Third-class carriages, being forbidden ground, were much more exciting than first-class ones.

The train steamed out of the station. In her mind's eye was a pleasant vision of Aunt Marcella, dignified but furious, searching the platform for her errant niece and finally receiving the note from the obliging porter with the flowing moustache. Then—then— Felicity's blue eyes danced and she gave a delicious little gurgle.

"Nebuchadnezzar in his rage and fury won't be in it," she said aloud.

"I beg your pardon," said a voice from the other corner of the carriage.

Felicity turned with a start. She had been so lost in her dreams that she had not heard anyone enter the carriage.

A young man sat on the seat by the other window. He was neither handsome, nor well dressed, but he had an unmistakable air of breeding. And Felicity decided that though he was ugly it was a nice kind of ugliness. He looked like a rough-haired fox terrier, and Felicity liked rough-haired fox terriers. His eyes were honest and kindly and humorous, and he had a nice smile. Felicity summed people up quickly. Despite her youth no one could be more haughtily chilling than Miss Norma Felicity Montague Harborough when she liked. But the look she turned on the young man was friendly.

"What did you say?" she said.

"I thought you spoke to me," said the young man.

"No. I was speaking to myself," said Felicity. "I didn't know you were there. I said: 'Nebuchadnezzar in his rage and fury won't be in it.' I was thinking about Aunt Marcella."

"Oh!" said the young man.

"You see," said Felicity, becoming expansive under the influence of her late successful *coup* and the kindly amused sympathy in the young man's eyes, "I've just entered into another stage. A new chapter of my life opens to-day. I have put away childish things, as Shakespeare says."

"Not Shakespeare," said the young man. "St. Paul."

"Well, St. Paul then," said Felicity impatiently. "I knew it was someone beginning with S."

"Paul doesn't begin with S," said the young man.

"No, but Saint does," said Felicity. "Anyway, that's why I feel so excited. I've done Aunt Marcella in the eye and I've begun a fresh chapter in my life all on the same day."

"You know, that's a strange coincidence," said the young man. "Because I, too, am beginning a new chapter of my life to-day."

Felicity looked him up and down.

"You're too old to be just leaving school," she said.

"Yes," he said. "I've just got a job."

"Your first?" said Felicity with interest.

He laughed.

"Lord, no! My first was the War. I went to it straight from school. I just got in for the tail end of it. Got off with a gammy leg. I'd meant to go to Cambridge, but— well, I won't bore you with my life story."

"Oh, please go on," said Felicity, leaning forward, her elbow on her crossed knee, her exquisite little face resting on her hands, her glorious plait over her shoulder. "Please go on. I love hearing the stories of people's lives."

"Well——." The young man looked out of the window.

"You see, my father had been killed in the War, and my mother's income considerably messed up, also through the War. So Cambridge was out of the question. I took a secretarial training, but"—he gave her his pleasant boyish smile—"there were thousands of men a jolly sight better than I, and without gammy legs, after all the jobs. I gave it up in the end, and got a job on the Gold Coast."

"What fun!" said Felicity. "Did you find gold?" He smiled.

"Far from it. I crocked up and the doctor sent me-home. I've been tramping round ever since trying to find someone ass enough to take me on as a secretary."

"I think you'd make a very good secretary," said Felicity, with an air of deep wisdom.

"Oh, I'm not bad," said the young man modestly.

"Anyway," said Felicity fervently, "I'm so glad you found someone."

The young man blushed, and for the first time looked a little confused.

"Well, I haven't—exactly," he said. "I mean—I've got a job, but it's not a secretarial job. It's—well, it's a job as a valet, but it's better than nothing."

Felicity again looked him up and down.

"You're too good for that," she said solemnly.

He laughed and bowed. His slight constraint had disappeared at once.

"Thank you for those kind words," he said. Then he went on cheerfully: "It's a job, anyway, with a real live salary—I mean wages. I'm too bucked for words to get it. You don't know what it's like cadging about after jobs day after day, especially when he stopped as though he had said more than he meant.

"Please go on," said Felicity earnestly. "Please tell me *everything*."

He laughed again.

"You're too sympathetic," he said. "You shouldn't draw people's life stories from them like this. It's bad for them. It makes them egotistical."

"Do you think I am sympathetic?" said Felicity seriously. "I'd love to know, because now I've left school I've got to decide what sort of a person to be. I'm torn between the intellectual sort and the sympathetic sort of person. They seldom go together. But it takes so much trouble being intellectual, don't you think? It's heaps easier to be sympathetic than it is to be intellectual."

The young man was watching her with twinkling eyes.

"And much nicer," he said.

"*And* more interesting," said Felicity. "Well, you'd got to 'especially when——' and then you stopped."

"I was going to tell you about my mother."

"Do tell me about your mother," said Felicity.

"Well—only that I've felt the vilest sort of a worm for living on her while I've been job hunting. She's an angel. I could talk all night and never make you understand what an angel she is. You—well, you know what mothers are."

"No, I don't," said Felicity, and the wistfulness of voice and eyes was real this time. "My mother died when I was born and my father died soon after. I've only got Aunt Marcella, who's more like an ostrich than an aunt, let alone a mother. Marcia was rather nice. She's my eldest sister. But now she's married, of course, she's more or less lost to us. I've got another sister, Rosemary, but she tries to boss me, and, of course, I can't put up with that."

"Of course," agreed the young man gravely.

"She's too pretty, too," said Felicity thoughtfully. "It makes them awfully conceited, you know."

"I suppose it does," said the young man.

"Then I've got a married brother, John, who's rather stuffy, and an unmarried brother, Ronnie, who's very nice, and that's all my family; but do go on about your mother."

"Well," said the young man, "she's not been well, and you know how you long to get them things when they're not well—grapes, and flowers, and wine, and nourishing things. It's been pretty rotten living on her when I ought to be cosseting her up, and when I got this job I nearly danced all the way home. With my first salary—I mean wage—I'm jolly well going to buy her all the ridiculous and extravagant and unnecessary things I can think of. You can understand the feeling, can't you?"

"Rather!" breathed Felicity. "Do go on."

The train was slowing down at Marleigh. The young man began to collect his bags.

"I get out at this station," he said.

"So do I," said Felicity.

"My job's here," said the young man. "I'm valet to Sir Digby Harborough, at Bridgeways Hall."

"What's your name?" said Felicity.

"Franklin," said the young man.

She held out her hand.

"Sir Digby Harborough's my grandfather, Mr. Franklin," she said. "I hope that we shall now see a lot of each other, and be *real* friends."

The look of amazement in his face gave place to amusement, and then to the whimsical seriousness with which he had treated most of her statements.

"We can't, Miss Harborough," he said. "You'll play the game by your grandfather, and so shall I. It wouldn't be cricket on either of our parts to be friends. But," he took her hand and grinned at her out of his friendly grey eyes, "you're a real sport."

He helped her down on to the platform. She looked round, and her speedwell-blue eyes twinkled demurely.

"I shall have to walk," she said. "There's nothing to meet me. You see, I gave Aunt Marcella the slip. At this moment she's probably having all sorts of hysterics on Paddington Station."

"Oh, yes—she's the one to whom Nebuchadnezzar in his rage and fury was nothing?"

"Yes."

"I gather," he said, "that you're in for a bad time when she returns."

"That all depends," said Felicity. Then she went on with great dignity: "One must show people that one is no longer a child. Well, we'll walk to the Hall, Mr. Franklin. Leave your bags to be sent on."

"We'll walk, Miss Harborough," he said, "but not together. I don't want to be unsociable, but neither do I want to lose my job."

The wistful corners of her pretty mouth hardened into obstinacy.

"You'll have to walk," she said firmly, "and I don't see how you can possibly prevent my walking with you. When all's said and done it's a free country."

"All right," he said; "but I see myself scanning the advert, pages of the *Daily Telegraph* before another sun has set. You know, I think the walls of Hades must be plastered with the advert, pages of the *Daily Telegraph*."

They had left the station and were swinging along a country lane.

"I'm a Socialist," said Felicity suddenly.

"Since when?"

"Since I met you."

"Oh, you mustn't let me influence you. I'm not a Socialist myself, but——"

"Oh, help!" said Felicity. "Here's Rosemary."

Two riders were coming down the lane, a young man with a weak chin and a small, cherished-looking moustache, and a girl who sat her gleaming chestnut mare superbly.

Felicity's prettiness may be described. Not so Rosemary's. No words could describe the gleam of the golden hair beneath the hard riding hat, the alabaster whiteness of the beautiful proud face, the deep blue of the eyes, the queenly carriage of the shapely head.

She had reined in her horse.

"Hallo, kid!" she called down to Felicity.

Then she turned to Franklin, looked at him with delicate eyebrows raised in disdainful surprise, seemed about to speak, changed her mind and cantered on with her companion.

Franklin looked after her. He had gone rather pale. Felicity, who was watching, said suddenly:

"Don't fall in love with Rosemary. It's such a painfully ordinary thing to do. Everyone does it."

He gave a short laugh. For the first time something bitter crept into his face as though for the first time he realised fully his position and all it entailed.

"I suppose they do," he said. Then: "Will she be angry with you for walking up with me?"

"I don't think so. The whole thing would bore her too much. She's horribly bored by things. I hope she does, though. It will be a test of my principles. I shall suffer for my faith, you know, like the early Christians. Wait a minute!" She stopped suddenly in the middle of the road. "I've just got an idea. You'd rather be a secretary than a valet, wouldn't you?"

"I would."

"Well, I don't see why grandfather shouldn't have a secretary. I'll suggest it to him."

"For heaven's sake, don't!"

"Oh, I'll be awfully tactful. I can be *frightfully* tactful when I like. Here we are!"

They had been walking up an avenued drive and now arrived at a large house—low, rambling and Elizabethan.

Franklin stopped.

"I say," he said, looking round. "I ought to find some sort of a side door, you know."

"Oh, nonsense!" said Felicity, sweeping up the steps.

Franklin followed her into a large dim hall with dull gleams of armour against its tapestried walls. A butler came forward as they entered.

"Good-afternoon, Moult," said Felicity, cheerfully. "I came down a little earlier than I'd arranged. Aunt Marcella and the luggage are following me. This is Mr. Franklin, grandfather's new valet. We're simply famished. You might get tea for us in the drawing-room at once, please."

Moult turned red and moistened his lips. He seemed to be controlling his emotions with difficulty.

"Tea is laid for Mr. Franklin, miss," he said, duly respectful, "in the servants' hall, miss."

Felicity wandered into the drawing-room. Rosemary lay on the Chesterfield reading a novel.

"Rosemary," said Felicity, "I wish you'd help me about Franklin."

"After your disgraceful performance the other day," said Rosemary in her musical drawl, "I don't know how you dare mention his name. I'm surprised that grandfather didn't dismiss him at once as aunt wanted him to."

"But, Rosemary darling, listen. He's *much* too good to be a valet. He told me his life story in the train and——"

Rosemary turned back to her novel with a little groan. "Please spare me!" she said.

Felicity spared her and went disconsolately out of the room.

Franklin had been valet at the Hall now for a week. Sir Digby Harborough was completely satisfied with him. Not so Sir Digby

Harborough's youngest granddaughter. He had refused to assist Felicity along her self-chosen path of Socialism. He passed her in the corridors with lowered or averted eye. When she addressed him he answered, "Yes, miss," "No, miss," with expressionless face. He did not look happy. He looked determinedly cheerful and philosophical but not happy. He looked as if he were finding his position harder than he had expected. And his limp as he swung awkwardly about the great house pierced Felicity's tender heart. She could not rid herself of a feeling of responsibility for him. With youthful, warmhearted impulsiveness she had offered him her friendship, and with youthful, warm-hearted loyalty she refused to take it back, though he declined it a dozen times a day. It troubled Felicity. Rosemary might have helped, of course, but Rosemary was a spoilt beauty, and spoilt beauties weren't much good at helping.

She went across to the library where her grandfather always worked in the mornings and knocked at the door.

"Come in!"

The tone in which Sir Digby Harborough uttered (though uttered is but a mild way of putting it) those two words proclaimed to all the world that it was one of his bad days. Sir Digby Harborough suffered from the Harborough gout and the Harborough temper. Aunt Marcella was proud of both the gout and the temper. She would have felt ashamed of any elderly relative of the male sex who did not possess both the gout and the temper. Common people might be immune from such things. Not so the Harboroughs. As long as history itself existed there had existed the Harborough gout and the Harborough temper.

In appearance Sir Digby was very red as to the face and very white as to the moustache and very fierce as to the eyes. Sir Digby could burst out on occasions into such aristocratic blue-blooded rage that the very furniture in his vicinity trembled.

Sir Digby was engaged in attending to his morning's correspondence. This ceremony generally occupied his whole morning, and provided much exercise for the Harborough temper.

He was surrounded by envelopes and notepaper.

"Fools!" he sputtered, as Felicity opened the door. "Confounded imbeciles!"

Felicity came into the room and sat on the edge of his desk, watching him calmly.

He tore open another letter.

"The only sensible one of the bunch," he growled, handing it to her when he had read it, "from a Professor Foxton, of Leeds University, wanting to come over and see my manuscripts and show me his."

Sir Digby Harborough was a collector. The collection of miniatures in the blue parlour was famous throughout Europe. In the big drawing-room was a collection of early English china that connoisseurs came many miles to see. In his library was a collection of mediaeval manuscripts. To a fellow collector Sir Digby Harborough would unbend as to no one else. To a fellow collector Sir Digby Harborough was almost human.

"Shall I write the answer, grandfather?"

"NO!"

"You ought to have a secretary, you know, grandfather," she said tentatively.

It was an inopportune remark at an inopportune moment. Sir Digby Harborough had just shaken his fountain pen to see if there was any ink in it. It had replied in the affirmative with joyous abandon, spattering with ink all the notepaper within its reach. Sir Digby Harborough went from red to purple and turned with fury upon the only human being available.

"Get out!" he roared at Felicity

Felicity got out.

It was a hot day. A thin, scholarly-looking gentleman panted up the drive to the front door of Bridgeways Hall. Like Felicity a week before, he had arrived by an earlier train than was expected. Sir Digby Harborough had ordered that stately, prehistoric, coat-of-armed equipage known to Felicity and Rosemary as "the family hearse" and to Moult as "the kerridge" (Sir Digby disliked motors) to meet the later train, but as Professor Foxton arrived early it was not needed. Sir Digby was not quite ready to receive him, so he was shown into the blue parlour while Sir Digby, puffing, important, excited, arranged his collection of mediaeval manuscripts to their best advantage. Then Moult ushered the visitor into the library.

As Professor Foxton crossed the hall from the blue parlour to the library he noticed two people. A very pretty girl with blue eyes and a long plait of red-gold hair was sitting on a high monk's chest dangling gleaming black silk-clad legs and reading a novel, and a man was crossing the back of the hall. The man was dressed like a gentleman's gentleman, but somehow didn't look like one; only succeeded in looking as if he were trying to look like one. So much Professor Foxton saw in one lightning glance before the library door closed on him and Sir Digby Harborough came forward with outstretched hand to greet him.

The gentleman's gentleman, who had returned Professor Foxton's scrutiny with unusual keenness, hesitated, with his hand on the green baize door that led to the kitchen regions, then turned back and approached the pretty schoolgirl.

"Who was that?" he said shortly.

Felicity stared. It was the first time he had addressed her as a human being since their journey from London.

"A Professor something, of somewhere," she said. "Why?"

"Professor who, of where?" he insisted.

She considered with frowning brows.

"Oh, yes, I remember," she said, "Professor Foxton, of Leeds University."

"Stay here a minute," he said, "I'm just going to telephone."

He went to the recess at the further end of the hall and Felicity returned to her book.

"Are you sure it was Foxton, of Leeds?" he said abruptly.

"Sure. I saw the letter."

"Professor Foxton, of Leeds University, is in Switzerland."

Her speedwell-blue eyes opened wide.

"Then who's this?" she said.

"That's what I want to know," he said, still frowning meditatively. "I've seen this chap before, but I can't think where."

"How exciting!" said Felicity. "*Do* think."

"I'm trying, to——"

Suddenly he slapped his thigh and said: "*Got* it! I say, where's he been? Anywhere beside the library?"

"Blue parlour."

"Miniatures there, aren't there? Go and see if they're all right. I'm going to telephone again."

Felicity rose, smiling at him with lazy mischief.

"You're rather forgetting the 'miss' this morning, aren't you?" she said.

He grinned back at her. He looked young and alive again. The air of forced, dogged servility of the last week had dropped from him.

"Blow the 'miss,'" he said.

He joined her in the blue parlour some minutes later.

"Well?" he said.

"Four gone," she said slowly, "the four best ones. Someone's forced the case, and—and—look—the window's right open at the bottom and muddy footmarks all round it. Someone must have got in through the window."

He shrugged his shoulders.

"I wonder," he said.

"Anyway, let's go and tell grandfather," said Felicity.

The party returned to the library from their investigation in the blue parlour.

Sir Digby, purple-faced and incoherent with rage; Professor Foxton, suave and sympathetic, followed by Felicity and Franklin.

"I wouldn't know the fellow again if I saw him," said Professor Foxton, "but I remember noticing him skulking in the bushes just outside the window. I only regret not having warned you, but it occurred to me that perhaps he was some under-gardener. He must have opened the window and taken them as soon as I left the room."

"We must get the police in," shouted Sir Digby, "There's no time to lose."

Franklin spoke for the first time.

"I took the liberty of sending for the police as soon as I discovered the theft, sir," he said quietly.

Professor Foxton threw him a quick glance. He found the young man's gaze disconcerting. He bundled his manuscripts into his bag. His manuscripts had proved singularly trivial and uninteresting, but that had rather endeared him to Sir Digby than otherwise. Sir Digby preferred having his own treasures admired to admiring other people's. This is a not uncommon trait among collectors.

"Well," said Professor Foxton, as he fastened up his bag and took out his watch, "I'm due at a lecture in town in an hour's time and I must fly to my train. I could be no further use to you if I stayed. I can only assure you of my sympathy and say how sorry I am that such a pleasant visit should terminate in this way. But it has been, sir, an education to see your wonderful collection of manuscripts. Good-bye."

He held out his hand to Sir Digby.

Suddenly Franklin stepped forward.

"As the only person known to have been alone in the blue parlour this morning, sir," he said blandly to the professor, "I'm sure you'll have no objection to turning out your pockets."

There was a sudden tense silence. Sir Digby's face turned a deep purple, but the visitor only smiled, though a close observer might have noticed that there was something suddenly alert and on guard behind his amusement. He turned to Sir Digby.

"Is this your secretary, Sir Digby?" he said.

"No, my valet," said Sir Digby.

Professor Foxton raised his eyebrows.

"Really?" he said. "From his manner, I thought——However, the young man's suggestion is a sensible one. Somehow," he smiled again, "it never occurred to me that I might be accused of the theft."

"This is outrageous, sir!" thundered Sir Digby to his valet.

"Oh, but I most assuredly must conform with the suggestion now that it has been made," said the professor, still smiling.

As he spoke he began to turn out his pockets. The valet watched him closely, unperturbed by his master's fury.

"And your bag?" he said pleasantly.

"Get out of the room!" thundered Sir Digby. "I dismiss you from my service, sir. Do you hear me?"

The valet took no more notice of the order than if it had been the cooing of a dove.

"The bag?" he said again.

As he spoke he turned it upside down and the manuscripts fell on to the table, leaving it empty. There was no trace of the miniatures. The valet took a penknife from his pocket. Then something strange seemed to happen to the professor's expression. The smile dropped from it. Something purposeful and desperate took its place. He made a lightning spring towards the open window, but Franklin was too quick for him. He caught him by the wrists and held him as if in a steel trap.

"Rip open the bottom of that bag," he said to Felicity.

Sir Digby was now past speech. He was mopping his brow with a large silk handkerchief.

Felicity cut away the lining of the bag.

Beneath it were the stolen miniatures.

"Gad!" ejaculated Sir Digby, and then feeling some further expression necessary he said again: "*Gad!*"

Two policemen passed the window on their way to the front door. The professor made a final desperate, unsuccessful struggle. Felicity closed and fastened the window.

"All right," said the professor to Franklin, "you can ease off. I know when I'm done." Franklin released his wrists. "Well, I quite enjoyed the old boy's gassing and I thought I'd brought it off, but you never know. We all have rotten luck at times." Then the police entered.

"I remembered his face," said Franklin half an hour later.

"But at first I couldn't think where I'd seen it. Then I remembered. He was in my company at the beginning of the war. He'd been had up for theft and had been let off on condition he joined up. He deserted after a few months of it. Then I saw in the paper not long ago that he'd been imprisoned again. He can't have been out long."

Sir Digby uttered a growl expressive of interest and gratitude and exhaustion and gout.

Then Moult entered with a pile of letters on a tray.

"The evening post, sir," he said.

He laid them down on Sir Digby's desk and disappeared. Sir Digby groaned. It was the last straw. He hated letters and he hated his fountain pen and he was tired and he had gout.

"Perhaps I could see to them, sir," said Franklin.

An hour later Felicity entered the room. Franklin sat at a small writing table near Sir Digby's desk, writing.

"I've finished these, sir," Franklin was saying.

"Write one more," growled Sir Digby. "Write out an advertisement for a valet."

"I thought I was——" began Franklin.

"Haven't you got ears in your head, man?" growled Six Digby. "I dismissed you from my service this afternoon."

"Then——"

"Was your father Maurice Franklin?"

"Yes, sir."

"Something about you reminded me of him when you were tackling that villain. I hadn't thought of it before. He was at Harrow."

Yes, sir."

"He was my fag there. Did he send you to Harrow, too, or," suspiciously, "did you go to one of those confounded, second-rate places like Eton?"

"No, sir," smiled Franklin. "I went to Harrow."

"*Felicity!*" stormed Sir Digby suddenly.

"Yes, grandfather?"

"Find that ass Moult and tell him to tell them to lay another place at dinner, as my secretary dines with us."

Chapter Two

Three Birds with One Stone

"You know, you're for it this time, Pins!" said Franklin. "As sure as I'm your grandfather's secretary, you're for it this time."

He was sitting at his desk in the library sorting out Sir Digby's correspondence. Felicity sat on her grandfather's unoccupied desk, swinging shapely, gleaming, black silk-enclosed legs. Her thick red-gold plait hung over her shoulders. Her speedwell-blue eyes were innocent and reproachful. She wore her stained-glass window expression.

"Frankie dear, I didn't really do anything," she said, in a voice of patient sweetness.

"Oh, no," said Franklin. "You only led an aged and eminent dignitary a will-o'-the-wisp dance over the highways and byways of Marleigh till midnight. Nothing, of course—absolutely nothing. But the story has got out and has come to the ears of certain members of the family—notably your aunt, Lady Montague"—Felicity groaned—"and your married brother John" —Felicity groaned again—"and they have come to the conclusion that something must be done about it."

Dancing devils of mischief chased the injured innocence from Felicity's eyes.

"It was such fun," she said, with a little gurgle of laughter. "If you'd *seen* him, Frankie! You know, you've been listening to my enemies' accounts of it. You've never heard mine. You ought to hear mine . . . He was coming to speak on total abstinence in Marleigh, and I know Ronny disapproves of total abstinence. Well, Ronny's my own beloved, favourite brother, and I've got to uphold him, haven't I? I disbelieve in it myself if it comes to that."

"Tch! Tch!" said Franklin reprovingly. "Now I hope you haven't been going the pace with the iced lemonade, Pins."

"Don't interrupt," said Felicity severely. "Anyway, he came, and Lady Deveret's motor that was to have met him had broken down on the way and there was nothing and no one to meet him. However, the station-master told him that it was only a few minutes' walk to the village hall, so he very bravely set off on foot. I don't believe he'd ever set off anywhere on foot in his life before. Then he met me."

"Ah," breathed Franklin; "now we're getting to it."

"Don't interrupt, Frankie," said Felicity again. "You put me out . . . He smiled a fat smile at me and he said in a fat voice: 'Can you direct me to the village hall, my little maid?' Yes, he really did. He said 'my little maid.' He only didn't put his hand on my head because he couldn't reach. Then I looked at him. He was fat beyond the dreams of fatness. He'd got the look of a person who rolls about fatly in fat motor-cars all day. Well, I looked at him and I imagined him strolling fatly down to the village hall (it was just round the corner) and talking fatly about total abstinence to a ghastly crowd of cranks who'd assembled to hear him and then rolling fatly off home to a too large supper (one could see he'd just had a too large dinner) and sleeping till about ten in the morning. He looked like that. So it occurred to me what a far, far better thing it would be to take him for a good long walk than let him spout rubbish about total abstinence.

"So I told him that I was going to his lecture myself and I'd show him the way and—Frankie, I took him right away from the village and across country five miles to Upper Marleigh. I pretended afterwards that I thought the lecture was going to be at Upper Marleigh. I was awfully nice and apologetic about it—afterwards. At first he quite enjoyed it—for the first quarter of a mile or so. He talked about total abstinence and said that I reminded him of a dear departed friend of his! Then he stopped talking and began to puff and perspire. Frankie, he *did* puff and perspire. I've put years on to that man's life. I've taken pounds of superfluous fat off him. I took him over two ploughed fields just to take that spick and span look off his boots. I got him muddied up to the knees. I said that it was a short cut. When we got there we found that the lecture wasn't to be held there at all, but down at Marleigh, and that there was no trap or taxi to be hired anywhere.

"It was a terrible moment for him, Frankie. He sat down on the grass by the roadside just outside the village pub and took his boots off. Just for that moment he was almost human. Like a tramp. I was quite nice to him. I told him how sorry I was. He didn't say much. He just moaned that he'd never get over it—never. He said that over and over again.

"I was almost sorry for him, Frankie. However, the shades of night were falling fast, so I admonished him a little and then went into the pub and got him a glass of beer. He drank it off without a word. Then I went and got him another glass, and he drank that off without a word. Then he asked what it was, and when I said beer he said he wouldn't have drunk it if he'd known, because he was a total abstainer. He said he'd thought it was lemonade. I said that perhaps it was lemonade, and he seemed comforted.

"Then he put on his boots again and off we started. He'd cleaned them up with grass, so I had to take him through the ploughed fields again. He left little rivulets of perspiration behind him. It was almost dark when we got home. When he was getting over a stile at the bottom of the hill he trod on a cow and said 'Damn!' Quite a lot of expression in it, too! And he didn't even apologise. You know, he ought to be grateful to me for the rest of his life. I turned him into a real live man for a whole evening. A ten-mile walk, two glasses of beer, and a 'damn.' I've given him something to remember in his old age.

"Anyway, we got down to Marleigh again, and he said that he didn't think he'd go to see the vicar or anyone. He didn't feel up to it. He'd write and explain. We went to the station and found a train just starting to town, so he got into it. He said his feet were causing him indescribable agony. Just as the train was going off he asked me rather anxiously if he smelt of lemonade. He seemed much relieved when I said he didn't. We parted without bitterness, though he didn't actually say he'd enjoyed it. But he looked quite perceptibly thinner. Anyway, that's the end of the story."

"Not quite," said Franklin drily. "The story got about somehow, and, as I said, your brother John heard about his wild young sister's leading an eminent dignitary over hill and dale——"

"And Johon," continued Felicity, "being Johon," she pursed up her mouth, folded her hands and imitated to perfection her elder brother's precise enunciation, "was shocked."

"Exactly! So John communicates with your aunt——"

"Oh dear!" sighed Felicity.

"And the result," continued Franklin, "is that he is coming down to confer with your aunt and your sister as to what is to be done about it."

"Oh, Hades!" said Felicity.

"And the conference is to take place to-morrow."

"Oh, and——"

The door opened suddenly, and Rosemary entered, followed by a tall thin man with a sallow face and an unpleasant mouth hidden by an over-cultivated moustache.

Rosemary went up to Felicity. She ignored her grandfather's secretary. Or rather, she acknowledged him only by a lowering of her white lids and an almost imperceptible curl of her beautiful lip. Rosemary, as a rule, treated her grandfather's employees graciously. But she did not treat her grandfather's secretary graciously. It was as if some antagonism had sprung up between them at their first meeting and had grown stronger ever since.

"My sister Felicity," she said. "Lord Rowman."

Felicity looked up and down the thin figure. Her eyes rested finally on the little sneering mouth behind its covering moustache. Then she inclined her head very haughtily. The chattering schoolgirl of a few minutes ago had vanished completely. She was Miss Norma Felicity Montague Harborough, endowed with her due share of the famous Harborough haughtiness. Rosemary and the man went over to the window.

"This is the view I told you about," said Rosemary in her sweet, drawling, indolent voice. "You can see three counties from this window."

The man's little eyes were fixed on the perfect lines of her profile.

"It's certainly a beautiful view," he said meaningly.

She knew what he meant but she showed neither pleasure nor resentment, only that supreme boredom that was her usual attitude to everyone and everything. Without looking at Felicity or Franklin again, she swept from the room, followed by her cavalier.

"Well," said Felicity, as the door closed behind them, "what a fish! That's a new one, isn't it? It's jolly hard to keep up with them!"

Franklin's mouth was tight.

"If you want to know all about him," he said slowly, "he's a rotter, but he's rich and belongs to a family nearly as old as yours. His father married an American millionairess, and now they're both dead and this fellow's got it all. He's Society's most eligible *parti*."

"And I suppose he's in love with Rosemary?"

"One presumes so."

That night Felicity woke up with a start. She had gone to bed early and fallen asleep at once. At first she could not think what had roused her, then she saw Rosemary standing motionless at the window like a beautiful ghost in her white wrapper, looking down upon the moonlit garden.

"Rosemary!"

Rosemary turned slowly.

"What's the matter?" said Felicity.

"Nothing," said Rosemary. "I couldn't sleep. So I just—came in."

"Goodness! You did give me a shock! I thought you were a ghost! What time is it?"

"Just about one."

"Heavens, to-morrow morning! Let me see, what was going to happen to-morrow? Oh, I remember. They're going to meet in council to discuss the scandal of me and the dignitary."

Rosemary did not speak or move. She stood as if carved in marble, her wonderful eyes still fixed on the window.

"The only thing I do hope," said Felicity, "is that Aunt Marcella doesn't come and take up her quarters here. I believe she'd love to. She'd have larger scope for bossing than at the Dower House."

"Oh, she's going to come for a time," said Rosemary slowly. "She may make you the excuse. But she's going to come and chaperone. You see, grandfather won't be back for another fortnight, and Lord Rowman's going to come and stay here next week."

"Is it all arranged?"

"I believe so."

"Well, then, once she gets here she'll stick here, and how will you like that?"

"I don't suppose it will make much difference to me."

"Are you going to marry this Lord Rowman?"

"Why not?"

"People say he's a rotter."

The still, beautiful figure outlined in the moonlight shrugged its shoulders faintly.

"People could say that about most men. He's rich. He could give me the sort of things that I can't live without. I'm sick of being poor."

"We aren't poor."

"We are. You don't know what you're talking about. Lord Rowman could buy us up ten times over and not feel it."

"But, Rosemary"—Felicity sat up in bed, her arms on her hunched-up knees, her chin on her arms, her plait hanging over her shoulders, her eyes dreamy—"but, Rosemary, does it matter about a person being rich? I mean, if someone jolly and kind and——"

Rosemary interrupted her.

"The novelette hero, you mean," she drawled; "good, and kind, and true, and brave? He doesn't exist in real life, my child."

"But—Frankie——"

"Please," drawled Rosemary coldly, as she drew her dressing-gown about her, "spare me a eulogy on Mr. Franklin. Good-night!"

*

The family council had assembled, and was conferring in the library. Felicity had at first decided to play truant for the day, then she had come to the conclusion that it would be more entertaining to stay. So when she was summoned to the library she went with large, innocent, wondering blue eyes behind which danced the little devils of mischief.

Her elder brother John sat in the armchair by the fireplace. Lady Montague, Felicity's aunt, sat next to him. Rosemary, exquisite and bored, sat limply on the window-seat, gazing down at the terrace.

"Where does the corpse sit, Mr. Coroner—or shall I stand?" said Felicity pleasantly to her elder brother.

"Felicity," said John gravely, "this is no subject for levity."

John was a lawyer and a Member of Parliament. He was very thin, and precise, and judicial. His glance—even when he was only wishing you good-morning—was always stern and accusing. He had a little clinging wife called Violet who adored him, and no children. He had not brought his wife to-day as he had come upon what he termed an "unpleasant duty."

Felicity sat down in the vacant armchair, sprawling her slim, shapely young body in a manner that offended, indescribably, Lady Montague's ladylike taste.

"In our family," began John, in his best public manner, resting his elbows on the arm of his chair and making his finger-tips meet, "we have always set our faces against allowing our young people to be brought up with that utter lack of restraint or discipline which is a characteristic of the age; but in your case we have, I am afraid, neglected our duty."

"Felicity darling!" murmured Lady Montague, unable any longer to restrain herself. "I can see your—er— knees!"

"Yes, I know," said Felicity. "I've got rather nice knees."

"When I heard about your escapade last week," went on John, "when I heard of your deliberately misdirecting a worthy public man, who is also a dear friend of my wife's father—I give you the credit, my dear girl, of not knowing that——"

"No, I didn't," admitted Felicity; "but it does make it more interesting."

"When I heard that," said John, "I realised how we had—er—neglected our duty in making no arrangement for your—er—your—your *menage*"—John felt that that was not quite the right word, and hurried on—"during this year between your leaving school and your coming-out. Your aunt has her own duties, of course, which amply occupy her time, and your sister"—with a courteous bow in the direction of his beautiful, unresponsive sister, who was still staring dreamily down at the terrace (John respected Rosemary's social success)—"has her innumerable social calls, and grandfather, of course, is—er—is also too busy to attend to the matter."

"Your style's going off, John," murmured Felicity sadly "Anyone might say, 'attend to the matter.'"

John ignored the interruption.

"So we have discussed the matter in all its bearings, and we have decided that, subject to grandfather's consent, your aunt should employ some lady who will supervise your studies and accompany you on your walks and—er——"

"Chaperon the dignitaries?" supplied Felicity.

"Er—supervise your studies," said John, who liked to have the last word.

"It all sounds simply ripping," said Felicity. "I can't tell you how grateful I am to you all. The only thing I'm doubtful about is whether the lady aunt chooses would really care for me. I have a sort of feeling that I mightn't be her sort. I suggest that you let Frankie and me choose the lady."

"I'm sure," said John patiently and courteously, "that Mr. Franklin would be the first person to realise that he is quite unfitted for such a—er—transaction. Your aunt will choose the lady. She will also take up her residence here for a few weeks till the—er—arrangement is—er—in full working order."

"Frankie, do you realise that the momentous day has arrived?"

"I realise," said Franklin patiently, "that you're sitting on the papers I want. They're important papers connected with the estate, and you aren't doing them any good."

"Don't be a gross materialist! I want your whole attention, and

I'm not going to move. Now listen, Frankie. To-day three people are going to arrive and dash to the ground our cups of happiness. First of all, there arrives Miss Bloke! It's a vulgar name, isn't it? But she's not vulgar! Oh, dear, no!"

"And who's Miss Bloke?"

"Don't you know? She's the companion-chaperon-instructress chosen by Aunt Marcella to bring my red hairs in sorrow to the grave."

"She may be nice!"

"She mayn't! I've just seen her photograph!"

"What does she look like?"

"She looks a perfect lady. I shall never be able to bear her. And she's not only one! There will be three serpents in our Eden ere the sun sets, Frankie!"

"Oh, you mean——"

"I mean Aunt Marcella, who arrives some time before lunch. That's a pity, you know, because we're going to have pheasant, but Aunt Marcella's presence will take away my appetite, and I shan't be able to do justice to it. Then the third serpent is Lord Rowman. Rosemary is going to marry him because he's got a lot of money. You know, Frankie"—she brought out a purse from her pocket, and from the purse a pound note—"I'd give this—all that's left of what brother John generously gave me when he came down here messing up my life last week—I'd give it gladly if there could be three separate accidents to the three serpents on their way down to-day."

"I say, Pins," said Franklin, "don't do anything rash, will you?"

Into Felicity's eyes came that innocence and meekness that those set in authority over her had learnt to dread.

"If I could think of anything to do," she said dreamily, "I'd do it!"

"Thank Heaven you can't!" said Franklin.

"All we can hope for," said Felicity, "is that Fate will open out a way for us."

"As long as you don't start monkeying with Fate——"

"You're unsympathetic, Frankie. You're ruffled because Lord

26

Rowman's coming. You've not your nicest side out at all. Here are your nasty old papers. I'll leave you to your materialism. Good-bye!"

Half an hour later Felicity thrust her head through the library window.

"She's come."

"Who's come?" said Franklin absently, without looking up from his work.

"Blokie, of course, darling. I've seen her in the distance."

"What's she like?" said Franklin.

"She's worse than your wildest nightmare, Frankie. She only doesn't wear elastic-sided boots because they aren't manufactured nowadays, I'm going to drown myself in the village pond."

"Not the pond, Pins," pleaded Franklin. "It's so dirty. Do try to think of a cleaner death."

"All right," said Felicity cheerfully. "I'll hang myself from the tallest pine-tree on the mountain-side. That'll be more poetical, too. You'll send a wreath to my funeral, won't you?"

She swung off, whistling. She hoped that Miss Bloke could see her swinging and hear her whistling. She went down to the main road and past the village. Just outside the village a car passed her, and in it she saw the sallow features and over-developed moustache of Lord Rowman "Oh, lord," she groaned, "now all the three of them will be there! Ours'll be a nice 'ouse, ours will!"

She turned the bend in the road and stopped short. A green caravan stood by the roadside, and near it was a man sitting in the shadow of the hedge smoking a pipe. Felicity's eyes went from the caravan to the man and from the man to the caravan. She liked the caravan and she liked the man. The caravan was a most fascinating shade of green and the man had a humorous face with a turned-up nose and a mouth whose curves even in repose suggested a grin.

"Hallo!" said Felicity.

"Hallo!" said the man, taking his pipe out of his mouth and grinning at her "'Ot, ain't it?"

"Yes, ain't it?" agreed Felicity.

She sat down on the grass by the side of the man.

"What have you got in the van?" she said pleasantly. The man took his pipe out of his mouth again, grinned at her, and uttered the one word "hannymals." Then he replaced his pipe.

"Going to a circus?" said Felicity, with interest.

"No, miss," said the man. "I've been over to old Mr. Moxton's place in Mossbridge—taking hannymals to him."

"Oh, I know about him!" said Felicity. "He's *very* eccentric, they say. Did you find him eccentric?"

"*An'* I did, miss," said the man. "'E wrote to my boss—a dealer in hannymals my boss is; supplies curious pets to the haristocracy an' the stage. Top of the tree in that line, my boss is. There's no hannymal that my boss can't perduce—at shortest notice, too . . . Well, this here Mr. Moxton 'e wrote an' he said he wanted a snake an' a tiger cub an' a swearin' parrot, an' would we send a selection of each for him to choose from."

Felicity's musical laugh rang out.

"How lovely! And did you?"

"Well, miss," said the man proudly, "we've got our reppetation to consider. We sent two of each."

"Are—are they in the van?" said Felicity, breathless with excitement "One of each," said the man. "He's chosen the ones he wanted. I'm takin' the hother three back 'ome."

"Oh!" gasped Felicity. "Do let me look!"

She ran to the caravan and opened the door. The man rose slowly, knocked out his pipe, and followed her.

There they were in roomy cages inside the caravan—a green, evil-looking snake, an adorable little tiger cub, and a parrot with a glinting, cynical eye.

"Go right in an' look at 'em, miss," he encouraged her. "They won't do you any harm. That there snake he's called Judas, same as the Judas in the Bible—he's had his fangs took out an' he's as gentle as a lamb, though not because he wants to be, believe me. While Felix"—he pointed to the tiger cub—"Felix is as playful as a kitten." He opened the cage door and put in his hand. The tiger cub began to lick it and gambol about playfully. "'E's smart, too," went on the man affectionately. "Tricks he can do an' all—*fight,*

Felix," he commanded. The tiger cub bared his teeth and snarled, then darted round after a piece of straw like a kitten. "And here's ole Foxy"— he pointed to the parrot.

"He doesn't seem to be swearing much," said Felicity, disappointed.

"'E's all right so long as he's not covered up," said the man. "When he's covered up you'd 'ardly believe the words that bird knows, miss. It's somethink orful! It fair gives me the creeps sometimes!"

"Do cover him up," pleaded Felicity.

"No, miss," he said firmly, "you don't 'ardly know what you're askin', miss. You don't reely. I dunno where the bird picked 'em up. I almost has to put cotton wool in my ears sometimes. 'E's got to be covered else he doesn't sleep. But the first five minutes—well, it's a hedducation to listen to 'im. No, miss. I've never covered 'im up before a lady yet, an' I never will."

Felicity was not listening to him or looking at him. She was standing very still, the speedwell-blue eyes fixed dreamily on the far horizon, the lovely lips parted over small white teeth.

"It's Fate," she said at last, slowly.

"Beg pardon, miss?" said the man.

"I said it was Fate," said Felicity distinctly.

The man looked anxious.

"It is a bit 'ot, miss," he said. "I've known it affect people sudden-like before. S'pose you go an' sit down quiet a bit over there by the 'edge or——"

"Now, listen," said Felicity imperiously. "Would you like some—some beer or something, and something to eat and a nice rest for—say—two hours?"

The man was still looking at her anxiously.

"Wouldn't I?" he said jocularly. "Specially the beer. But you sure you're feelin' all right, miss?"

"Will you come with me," said Felicity, "up to the Hall and they'll give you some beer and a good meal and a rest, and you can go on later when it's cooler. Could you get back in time?"

"Yes," said the man; "but"—pointing to the caravan—"what about me hannymals?"

"They'll be all right," said Felicity. "Bring it along. I'll tell you just where to leave it."

He looked at Felicity. Felicity's eyes were blue limpid pools of innocence.

"Look here, miss," he said slowly, "do you want to go monkeyin' about with me hannymals?"

Felicity took out her purse and handed him her pound note.

"When you start off home," she said, "your animals will be just where you left them."

The man looked at Felicity, then at the note, then at the caravan. Then he looked back from the caravan to the note and from the note to Felicity. Then he took the note, folded it up, and put it into his pocket.

"Right you are, miss," he said.

"Now," said Felicity briskly, "let's get off home. Come along!"

He took the nose-bag off the horse. She seated herself on the low board in front; he took up the reins and they set off at a walk down the road, Felix growling softly inside the van. Felicity enjoyed the drive except for one thing. No one saw her. If Miss Bloke or her aunt had seen her her cup of happiness would have been full.

They entered the hall grounds by an inconspicuous gate. The caravan halted at Felicity's direction near a side door. Then Felicity took the man to the housekeeper's room. Mrs. French, the housekeeper, was a great friend of Felicity's. Mr. Moult, the butler, was not. Mr. Moult was a perfect gentleman and approved only of perfect ladies. Though he adored the family pedigree he had come reluctantly to the conclusion that Miss Felicity was not a perfect lady. Her behaviour pained him on an average a dozen times a day. He forgave her on the score of her youth, but he looked forward to her future with apprehension . . . So Felicity had learnt to look for no help from Moult . . .

"Mrs. French," said Felicity, with her most winning smile (and Felicity's most winning smile was a very decided winner). "This is Mr.——what is your name?" she said to the nice low man.

"Smith," said the nice low man.

"Smith, of course," said Felicity graciously. "This is Mr. Smith,

Mrs. French. He's a *great* friend of mine. I want him to have some beer and something to eat, and a nice rest for the next two hours. You'll be an angel and look after him, won't you?"

Mrs. French smiled her motherly, all-embracing smile. It embraced Felicity, and the nice low man, and the canary in the window, and every article of furniture in the room. That smile had never yet failed Felicity.

"Certainly, dearie," she said. "Don't you worry. I'll see to it!"

Felicity blew her a kiss and went out into the corridor. Then she stood for a moment, her brow drawn into a frown, one hand at her lips, the other on her hip, her glorious pigtail as usual over her shoulder. She needed a little more help here. Moult was no good. Lewis, the head footman, was no good. But James—James, the under-footman, adored her. James was young and romantic, and a smile from Felicity's blue eyes increased his pulse from normal to 100. Rosemary did not appeal to him. Rosemary was too arctic. And Rosemary never smiled at him. Felicity's brow cleared. She ran lightly down the corridor through the green baize door into the hall. There she rang the bell. James appeared.

"James," said Felicity, "I want you to help me. Will you?"

"Certainly, miss," said the devoted James.

"Without asking any questions or ever telling anyone about it?" Felicity smiled as she spoke and James' pulse leapt from normal to 100. He wished she'd asked him to fight giants or lions for her. Something really difficult.

"Certainly, miss," said James dizzily.

Lord Rowman had arrived, and was in the drawing-room talking with, or rather being talked to by, Lady Montague. He was not feeling his brightest and best. He had celebrated his last evening in town as an unencumbered bachelor (for he meant to return as the fiancé of the beautiful Miss Rosemary Harborough) by what was known to his lordship and his friends as a "jag to the *n*th." His morning headache was still a going concern, and the solid things of the world were still to his lordship's vision apt to appear unsteady. He was in a mood easily to feel annoyed. And he felt annoyed.

He'd arrived quite an hour ago and he'd seen no one but this harridan who was talking rock gardens to him (Rock Gardens—by gad!). Although everyone knew that he'd come down to propose to Rosemary, Rosemary had not yet appeared. He had been calmly told that she was out and would be in soon. That was cool cheek, thought his lordship. She knew he was coming. She ought to have been there to greet him, dressed in her prettiest frock and wearing her prettiest smile. And she wasn't. Confound her, she wasn't! He was boxed up instead with this Early-Victorian monument discussing—rock gardens. He'd thought of quite a lot of pretty things to say to Rosemary and instead he had to talk about rock gardens. Another thing that annoyed him was that he looked yellow. Every time he looked into a mirror (and there seemed to be a confounded lot of mirrors about the room) he saw himself looking yellow. And it annoyed him. He'd like to smash the beastly things.

"Saxifrages are so pretty, don't you think?" said Lady Montague. His lordship stood up, glared ferociously at his yellow countenance in the mirror over the mantelpiece and then turned to Lady Montague.

"I have some letters to write before tea," he snarled, "if you will kindly excuse me."

Lady Montague inclined her head majestically and smiled graciously.

"Certainly," she said. "Rosemary will probably be in by tea-time."

He began to smile, then caught sight of his yellow face again in the mirror and scowled instead.

He went up to his bedroom. Now Felicity had chosen the snake for Lord Rowman simply because she considered it the most suitable. To do Felicity justice she had no idea that the snake was a reptile to which his lordship had a particular aversion.

He opened the bedroom door jauntily. He'd escaped from that monumental harridan, anyway. He could lie down till tea-time and try to get rid of his foul head.

He opened the door.

A great green snake was crawling across the red carpet.

His lordship's face went from yellow to green. He skipped back to the corridor and closed the door sharply.

"Snakes!" he said.

He looked round wildly. Croombs, his valet, was coming along the corridor. His lordship put his hand to his throat.

"Croombs!" he said weakly. "I'm seeing snakes. Great green snakes crawling over carpets. I'd better get home. I—I can't see snakes here!"

"Let me get you a drop of something, my lord," said Croombs solicitously.

"The trouble is I've had too many drops of something," said his lordship. "Croombs, open that door and see if you can see a green snake."

Croombs opened the door. His lordship had caught Judas on a voyage of discovery across the bedroom. By the time Croombs opened the door Judas had found a nice warm corner behind the radiator that just suited him, and was no longer visible.

"Is there a snake there, Croombs?" said his lordship anxiously.

"No, my lord," said Croombs; "how could there be?"

"Exactly," said his lordship, "how could there be? But I saw one. A nasty green thing crawling across the carpet. Heaven alone knows what I shall be seeing next. Croombs, pack up at once. We're catching the next train to town."

"Oh, there you are, Felicity!" said Lady Montague. "Where *have* you been?"

Felicity, stretched at length on the Chesterfield in the smoking-room, tried to look as if she had been there all the afternoon, and eyed her aunt warily. Lady Montague looked put out. Most decidedly put out. There was a streak of red across her ladyship's cheekbones that always accompanied the state of "put outness" with her ladyship. Also she breathed hard. When Lady Montague breathed hard you knew that something had happened.

"Did I hear a motor going or coming?" said Felicity with well-simulated sleepiness.

"Going!" snapped her ladyship. "Lord Rowman said he felt ill one minute and said he was summoned to town on urgent business the next. Behaved most curiously. Unfortunately he met Rosemary coming in just as he was going out and she was so annoyed by the way he was behaving that she wouldn't speak to him. Just walked past him. You know what Rosemary can be like. *Most* unfortunate—*most* unfortunate."

"However, I've been looking for you all afternoon, Felicity—it's all most tiresome. That Miss—Miss Bloke" (it certainly was an unfortunate name, thought her ladyship, irritably) "has been in the morning-room all the afternoon. I've had to entertain Lord Rowman (he was *so* much interested in rock gardens) and I haven't had time to see to her. Felicity dear, I want you to go to her now and show her the school-room where you're going to work, and your little sitting-room that she will share with you."

"Yes, aunt," said Felicity meekly.

After a considerable interval Felicity joined Miss Bloke in the morning-room.

Miss Bloke was very thin and very angular. She wore pince-nez, a pained expression, and a dress that Victoria the Great and Good would have looked upon with entire approval. Her hair was scraped back from her high-furrowed brow and dressed in a little bun half-way up the back of her head. She had been chosen by Lady Montague out of dozens of applicants as being Lady Montague's ideal of all that a governess should be. She held out a bony hand.

"So this is Felicity?" she said precisely. "Felicity— from a Latin word meaning happiness. I am sure, dear, that you and I will get on together beautifully. You stoop a little, darling, don't you? But we can soon remedy that. Felicity! Happiness! Very pretty. How Old are you, dear? Sixteen? Your skirt is just a lee-tle short for sixteen. But we can soon remedy that. You know, when your dear aunt persuaded me to come to you (a Scottish earl badly wanted me for his daughters, too, but the family was mixed up with trade, and I felt it wouldn't do) I knew that we'd get on well together. We will read and walk together—nice little gentle walks, I mean. I believe," wagging a forefinger playfully, "that my Felicity's been going out without gloves. But we can soon remedy that. A lady's hands, dear, are never tanned. Never. And——"

"Aunt asked me to show you the school-room," said Felicity.

"Certainly, dear, certainly!" said Miss Bloke briskly. "Let us visit the little sanctum where we will spend so many happy hours together."

The school-room window curtains were blue, and on a stool near them was a large parrot in a cage that was decorated by a blue bow to match the curtains.

"A parrot!" guessed Miss Bloke brightly.

"Yes," said Felicity; "we're all awfully fond of parrots."

As she spoke she carelessly drew the curtains across the cage.

It is impossible to reproduce in print the stream of profanity that issued from the shrouded wires.

"Merciful heavens!" gasped Miss Bloke, as she fled precipitately from the room.

"Grandfather teaches them to talk," said Felicity un-blushingly as she joined her outside. "He is awfully successful with them!"

Miss Bloke said nothing. She still looked rather shaken.

"Now shall we go and look at the sitting-room?" said Felicity, her spirits rising.

"Er—yes," said Miss Bloke, recovering herself with an effort.

It appeared that Felicity had to leave Miss Bloke in the morning-room while she went to see whether the sitting-room was ready to receive visitors. Soon, however, she returned.

"It's quite tidy, Miss Bloke," she said. "Are you ready to come?"

Miss Bloke said she was. They went there in silence. Some fine touch of assurance had vanished from Miss Bloke's manner.

The curtains of the pleasant little sitting-room were pink. Near them was a parrot in a large cage decorated with a pink bow to match the curtains.

"Another parrot," said Miss Bloke, with a mirthless smile.

"Oh, yes," said Felicity; "we have parrots in most of the rooms."

She drew the curtain lightly across the cage, and at the words that followed Miss Bloke fled, trembling, into the corridor. Even Felicity found them, as Mr. Smith had predicted, a "hedducation."

"That one talks very nicely, doesn't he?" said Felicity, innocently, as she joined her instructor. "Much better than the others."

"I must just sit down a minute somewhere!" gasped Miss Bloke. "I'm feeling rather faint."

"Let's go back to the morning-room," suggested Felicity. "There's a sofa there. I'll leave you quite alone to rest for a few minutes. Then I'd like to show you my bedroom."

Miss Bloke had scarcely had time to close her eyes when Felicity came to take her to her bedroom.

"I'm still feeling faint," said Miss Bloke. "D-did you say your grandfather—er—trained the birds, dear?"

"Yes," said Felicity with a bright smile, "but we're all awfully fond of them. They're delightful pets, and so intelligent."

Miss Bloke swallowed hard but said nothing.

"This is my bedroom," said Felicity, throwing open a door. It was a pretty little bedroom. Its window curtains were orange, and near them was a parrot in a large cage that was decorated with an orange bow.

Miss Bloke gave a low moan and fled from the room with her hands to her ears. Her nerves had gone completely.

"I'm going home," she sobbed. "I can't bear it. Never in all my life have I heard such expressions. It's a *wicked* place. I—I—I'm going home. I'm going to the Scottish earl. I'd—I'd rather have *trade* than profanity."

Coming out of her bedroom half an hour later, Felicity met her aunt. Lady Montague looked more put out than ever. The scarlet patch had spread from her cheekbones all over her face. Her breathing was suggestive of a motor-cycle with a defective silencer.

"Did I hear a motor going down the drive just now, aunt dear?" said Felicity.

"I simply don't know what's come over everyone!" said Lady Montague, tearfully. "She had wonderful testimonials. Not one of them mentioned that she was mad. They ought to have told me that she was mad. It simply wasn't fair to let her come like that. Mad! Raving! Almost dangerous!"

"Was she mad, aunt?" said Felicity wonderingly.

"Raving! She's just gone. She suffers from hallucinations. She came to me and said she couldn't stay in a house that had profane parrots in every room. Profane parrots in every room. Those are the very words she used. Profane parrots in every room! Have you ever heard of such a thing? You know, I'm getting too old to have all these upsets, Felicity. First, Lord Rowman behaving in that strange way, and then this woman talking about profane parrots in every room."

Lady Montague was going to her bedroom. Felicity accompanied her. Her ladyship opened her bedroom door, still talking. "She's mad. It wasn't *right*——"

She stopped with a start. On her bed was a tiger—a real live tiger. Felix was having a comfortable rest, but he heard the word "right" and mistook it for "fight." He bared his teeth and snarled. With a wild scream Lady Montague turned and ran downstairs faster than she had run anywhere in the last forty years. She ran into the smoking-room, locked the door, moved the sofa across the door, put up the shutters, and then had hysterics in comfort.

"It's all right, aunt," said Felicity, soothingly, when Lady Montague had come out of hysterics, removed the sofa and unlocked the door. "It was quite harmless. It had escaped from a van—er— just near. It's all right now."

"It's *not* all right, Felicity," said Lady Montague, sitting up with great dignity and smoothing her ruffled hair. "I'm upset. I'm more upset than I've been for years! I'm—I'm really ill! I'm going straight home. I'm *going* to stay in bed for a week. I'm not even going to stay to pack. I'm—I'm really upset. Please ring the bell and order the motor at once!"

"Yes, aunt," said Felicity meekly.

Felicity went into the library and took her usual seat on her grandfather's desk.

Franklin looked up from his desk.

"Well?" he said.

"Frankie, have you heard a lot of commotion this afternoon?"

"A fair amount."

"Have you heard three motors go past the window?"

"Yes."

"The first"—Felicity checked them off on her fingers— "the first was Lord Rowman going home. He's done for himself. Rosemary will never speak to him again. The second was Miss Bloke going home. She's going to the Scottish earl because she'd rather have trade than profanity. The third was Aunt going back to the Dower House. She's going to bed for a week."

Franklin laid down his pen and looked at her sternly.

"Felicity," he said, "what have you been up to?"

"I've been killing birds," said Felicity calmly. "I mean, proverbially speaking. I've been killing three birds with one stone. Fate played into my hand. Fate and Mr. Smith—and James, of course. When I think of all the things that might have gone wrong this afternoon and didn't—it makes me hot and cold all over. But it doesn't matter, because it didn't—thanks to Fate and Mr. Smith and James. It's a long story, Frankie. I'll tell you some time, but not now. I'm rather busy just now. You see, in half an hour Mr. Smith should start for home."

"Who's Mr. Smith?" said Franklin, patiently.

"He's a nice man, Frankie. Aunt wouldn't like him. He's low, but nice. Anyhow, he wants to start off home in half an hour, and I've temporarily mislaid two of his hannymals—a tiger and a snake. They're somewhere about the house. Do come and help me look for them!"

Chapter Three

Felicity and Socialism

Felicity awoke that morning with a distinct feeling that something was going to happen. Yet, so far as she knew, there was nothing that could possibly happen. On the contrary, the day promised to be more than ordinarily dull. Lady Montague was staying in the house, and in whatever house Lady Montague stayed things moved slowly. Nothing ever "happened" (in the true sense of the word) in the vicinity of Lady Montague. Things only "moved," and moved with Victorian decorum and stateliness.

Sir Digby was suffering from one of his periodic attacks of gout. During such times he stayed in his room, and though his stentorian voice could frequently be heard roaring at Crampton, his long-suffering valet, he himself rarely issued forth. When he did, of course, things hummed.

Rosemary was, as usual, away from home staying with friends.

Ronald, Felicity's favourite brother, seldom came to Bridgeways Hall. Ronald was an attractive young officer in the Guards and found the atmosphere of Bridgeways Hall a little too oppressive for his youthful spirits. He visited it usually only when his funds were in need of replenishing. Felicity adored him, and, to do him justice, he gave Felicity a good time whenever it was at all possible.

In the library Franklin sat down at a small desk and began to sort Sir Digby's correspondence. There was another large desk in the room which, Felicity thought, Franklin would have found more convenient. She suspected that he sat at the small desk because from it he could see the photograph of Rosemary that was on the mantelpiece. Rosemary's calm, beautiful face looked at him from the photograph as coldly as it did in real life. That, however, was a subject on which Felicity never teased him.

She sat on the desk by him, swinging her slim, shapely legs. "Have you had your hair permanently waved, Frankie?" she said, her laughing blue eyes fixed on his bent head. "Or do you go every fortnight?"

"I go every fortnight," he said. "Now, Pins dear, run away and play with your dolls. I'm going to be busy."

"What are these?" said Felicity, taking up a pile of letters. "Love letters or bills?"

"Begging letters," said Franklin.

Felicity opened the top one and read it in silence.

"This is terrible," she said at last. "I hope you're going to do something about it . . . a poor woman called Marie Smyth-Bruce with no money and no food, and suffers from chronic legs, and her landlord's going to turn her out into the street because she can't pay any rent— what are chronic legs, Frankie?—anyway, they sound nasty—and no money at all, she says, and the larder empty. How much are you going to send her, Frankie?"

"Nothing."

"Why not?" said Felicity.

Her blue eyes looked severe.

"They're all frauds, my child. It's going into the waste-paper basket with the others."

"Frankie, I'm disappointed in you. You're a nasty, cold-hearted, grinding miser."

He laughed.

"It's nothing to do with me, anyway. Your grandfather's orders are that begging letters are all to be put into the waste-paper basket."

"Then grandfather's a nasty, cold-hearted, grinding miser."

"Tut, tut!"

"Frankie, I've told you before that I'm a Socialist. Here you sit in—in the lap of luxury with every comfort around you." She looked about the desk vaguely. "Stamp-lickers and calendars and—and inkpots and everything like that," she looked him up and

40

down, "well clothed, with your hair nicely waved . . . well fed . . . with two lumps of sugar in your coffee . . . and you harden your heart against this poor woman. Frankie," earnestly, "how would you like to have chronic legs and no money and no food? Aren't you going to send her ten pounds?"

"No, I'm not. I bet you sixpence that she's got plenty of money and plenty of food."

"You'll be saying her legs aren't chronic next," said Felicity sternly. "I'm *convinced* her legs are chronic. I thought better of you than this, Frankie. I——"

Moult entered the room in his best manner. Moult as a butler was almost too perfect to be true. He gave you the impression of a very clever actor interpreting the part of a butler in a romantic comedy of high life . . .

"Her ladyship," he said primly to Felicity, "is confined to her room with a headache, and would like a few words with you in her bedroom."

Felicity entered her aunt's bedroom singing to herself.

"Felicity dear," said Lady Montague, without opening her eyes. "Please!"

Lady Montague lay majestically on her bed. She suggested a stately recumbent monument in the chancel of an old church. With a ruff round her neck and a little lion at her feet the resemblance would have been almost complete.

"Good-morning, aunt!" said Felicity cheerfully as she sat down. "How are you?"

"I am suffering, Felicity," said Lady Montague, with great dignity. "I am suffering, but I make no complaints." She peeped at Felicity through half-closed lids. "Felicity," she said faintly, "don't cross your legs!" Felicity uncrossed them.

"People do nowadays, aunt," she said.

"Not the best people," said Lady Montague crushingly.

"What are chronic legs, aunt?" said Felicity.

"Please don't be vulgar, Felicity!" said Lady Montague. Felicity sighed.

41

"I sent for you, Felicity," said Lady Montague, "because I find myself in a quandary."

"A quan——?" said Felicity.

"A dilemma," said Lady Montague.

"Oh, yes, I know," said Felicity, "a thing with horns." Lady Montague stretched out a languid hand for the pile of letters that lay on the table by her bed.

"A distant cousin of ours is arriving in England from Russia and wishes to come and see us. She says"—Lady Montague turned over the letter, then closed her eyes as if exhausted by the effort—"she says she will probably arrive in London by the twelve-thirty train at St. Pancras, and would like to be met there by one of us and accompanied to Marleigh, as she finds travelling in England so confusing. You follow me, Felicity?"

"Oh, yes," said Felicity; "but who's going to meet her?"

Lady Montague raised a hand to her head.

"That, Felicity," she said, "is the difficulty . . . Pass me my smelling salts."

Felicity passed them.

"I," went on Lady Montague, "am so prostrate that I cannot speak or see or move."

"I'm so sorry, aunt!" murmured Felicity sympathetically.

"It is impossible for me to contemplate going up to town. Your sister Rosemary is away staying with friends. She does not return until this afternoon. There remains——"

"There remains me—or is it I?" said Felicity. "Which is it? There remains me . . . There remains I . . ."

"Felicity, kindly refrain from anticipating me. I was about to observe that there remains you——"

"You's nice and safe, of course," said Felicity dreamily.

"And my first thought was to send you to meet Cousin Mary—escorted, of course, by Brown."

Felicity groaned.

"But, unfortunately," said Lady Montague, "Brown is also indisposed as the result, I gather, of—going on the roundabout at the village fair last night."

"How inconsiderate of Brown to be indisposed!" said Felicity, with mock indignation.

"Exactly, Felicity," said Lady Montague heartily. "Just what I said to Freen this morning. I said, 'Surely the woman has not reached her age without discovering whether she can or cannot take a ride on a roundabout with impunity.'"

"Which can you, aunt?" said Felicity, with interest.

"I have never considered it consistent with my dignity to ascertain. Brown is one thing, I am another. But to return, after deep thought—very deep thought and very serious thought—I have decided that you shall ring up your sister-in-law Violet"—Felicity made a grimace—"whom I can trust in every possible way, and ask her to meet you at the London terminus; that together you meet Cousin Mary, and that you then bring her back here. Violet will see you both off at the London terminus. That leaves the first portion of the journey—from here to London—to be performed alone.

"It is," continued Lady Montague solemnly, "entirely against my principles to allow a young girl of your age to travel alone and unescorted, but I think on this occasion there is perhaps no harm in it."

"What is Cousin Mary like?" said Felicity.

"That again is a difficulty——"

"Quite a herd of dilemmas," murmured Felicity.

"She has never been to England before. Her mother was a Russian. And we have no photograph of her recent enough to be any guide to identification. But doubtless, with Violet's help, you will identify her."

"Doubtless," murmured Felicity.

"You will, then, Felicity, first ring up Violet and ask her to meet you at the London terminus, then you will proceed there alone, and—Felicity——"

"Yes, aunt."

"Go first-class."

"Yes, aunt. Good-bye."

"Good-bye. Oh, and Felicity——"

"Yes, aunt."

"Don't lean out of the carriage window."

"No, aunt. Good-bye."

Felicity opened the door.

"Good-bye—oh, and Felicity——"

"Yes, aunt."

"Don't speak to any stranger."

"No, aunt. Good-bye."

Felicity closed the bedroom door.

"Felicity!"

Felicity groaned and opened it again.

"Yes, aunt?"

"Don't get out till the train's quite stopped."

Felicity closed the door and went out into the corridor. "Heaven above us!" she remarked feelingly to a bust of Sir Walter Scott that stood there.

Twenty minutes later Felicity stepped into the library, dressed in her outdoor things.

"I'm having a day out, Frankie," she said. "I'm going to perform the journey to town alone and unescorted"—she began to tick her sentences off on her fingers—"first-class, not leaning out of the carriage window, not speaking to strangers, and not getting out of the carriage till the train stops——"

Franklin interrupted her.

"What on earth is it all about, Pins?"

"Ah," she said mysteriously. "I'm supposed to ring up Sister-in-law Violet from Mayfair and meet Cousin Mary from Russia, but it's just possible I may forget that part of it." She blew him a kiss. "Good-bye, Frankie." In the train Felicity took out the letter signed "Marie Smyth-Bruce," and the mischief died out of her blue eyes. She took very seriously her recent conversion to Socialism and the fact that she had as yet done nothing to justify it weighed on her conscience. But she would justify it now. She would seek out this Marie Smyth-Bruce with the strange handwriting and chronic legs, and hold out to her the right hand of fellowship. She would, if necessary, suffer for her belief. There was every probability that her beliefs would not be encouraged at home and that she would provide yet another dilemma for poor Aunt Marcella. But still, that was Aunt Marcella's fault for being a hide-bound aristocrat. She, Felicity, was a Socialist, and she must live up to her principles.

She walked lightly down the London platform. A well-tailored youth with a weak mouth and no chin gave her an ogling smile as tribute to her beauty. He received in return from ice-blue eyes a glance of such freezing hauteur that for the minute (though only just for the minute) he felt the worm he was.

At the exit of the station Felicity halted. Cousin Mary weighed rather heavily on her conscience. Then, with an effort, she pushed Cousin Mary off her conscience. She had no time, she told herself sternly, for females who could not find their way across London without help. Cousin Mary must be left to her own resources. It would do her good. It would be much better for Cousin Mary's character than to meet her and pilot her across London. And Felicity, the Socialist, was bent on the rescue of Marie Smyth-Bruce, the sufferer from cruel landlords and chronic legs.

She gave the taxi man the address and leant back in her seat with a mixture of apprehension and elation in her heart. She'd show Frankie and her grandfather and the rest of them that she really was a Socialist. They wouldn't dare not to take her seriously once she'd rescued Marie Smyth-Bruce from cruel landlords and chronic legs.

The taxi stopped at a little house in a little street, and Felicity looked at it with interest as she paid the man his fare.

It was most satisfactorily dirty and dilapidated. It would have been rather disappointing to find Marie Smyth-Bruce in a clean and prosperous house.

A female with a squint and incipient beard opened the door. Felicity's heart sank. She hoped that this was not Marie Smyth-Bruce. She was prepared to love Marie Smyth-Bruce, but she felt that she could not love a squint and an incipient beard.

"Does Miss Smyth-Bruce live here?" said Felicity. "I am Miss Felicity Harborough, and I have called to see her."

The woman wiped her hands and face on her apron.

"Well, I'm——" she began in utter amazement as she looked up and down Felicity. "Well, I'll be——'old 'ard a minute, miss, I'll go an' tell 'er."

She disappeared up the narrow stairs still murmuring. "Well—I'll be——" and Felicity 'eld 'ard in the narrow hall below. There seemed to be a great amount of whispering and shuffling going on overhead. At last the squint and incipient beard descended and said: "Will you go hup now, miss. She lives in the room at the top of the stairs."

Felicity went up, and the door at the top of the stairs was promptly flung open to receive her, revealing Miss Smyth-Bruce. Words cannot do justice to Miss Smyth-Bruce. She was thin and tall and battered and dingy and blowsy, but with an overpowering air of derelict elegance. Her long, thin nose was indubitably red and her short thin hair was wispy. She wore a dress that in the dim and far-back ages, before it began to go the round of all the dress agencies in London, must have been a very star in the firmament of fashion. It swept. It trailed. Around it hung festoons of torn lace. Miss Smyth-Bruce had evidently hastily changed into her robe of ceremony with the help of the squint and incipient beard. She advanced upon Felicity with hand held high in air and a radiant smile which revealed teeth as battered-looking as the rest of her.

"How do you do, dear?" she said. "So good of you to call. Take a pew, won't you, dearie?"

Felicity took a pew. It was rather an unsteady pew, but she managed with an effort to recover her balance and take another.

"You wrote to my grandfather," began Felicity.

"I did indeed, dearie," affirmed Miss Smyth-Bruce, "an' trew it was in he very word, although I had to swallow my natural pride before I could bring meself to do it—me what's been brought up genteel an' honest, like you 'ave yourself, dearie, rejewced to habject poverty, an' threw no fault of me own."

She took out a handkerchief which had seen better days and dried one eye. The other was fixed keenly on Felicity.

Felicity didn't know quite what to say. The career of a Socialist was more difficult than she had thought. She murmured, "I'm so sorry," and Miss Smyth-Bruce continued.

"Rejewced to habject poverty with the landlord goin' to turn me out this very night because I've no money to pay the rent," she continued, sniffing. "It's a crewel life, dearie, for them as is 'elpless in the grip of circumstances hover which they have no control."

She drew a breath and wiped the other eye.

Felicity struggled desperately for some suitable comment, but she need not have troubled. Miss Smyth-Bruce's oratory was independent of suitable comments. She only paused for breath.

"An' me starving," she went pathetically on. "Me what's had nothing to eat for days." She pointed dramatically across the room to a cupboard. "My larder—empty!"

She took out the handkerchief again. It was unfortunate from Miss Smyth-Bruce's point of view that at that minute a little breeze came through the window and blew open the insecurely fastened cupboard, revealing a plentiful store of bread and butter and bacon and cheese and cake. But Miss Smyth-Bruce was not disconcerted

"As a larder," she said with dignity, "was of no use to me owing to me having no food to put in it, Hi kindly let one of the other lodgers use it. Do they pay me hanything for rent of it?" she asked rhetorically, throwing out her arms. "No! An' do I soil me conscience by hever touching their vittles? No! As the Bible 'as it—I starve in the midst of plenty."

Felicity felt her small murmur of sympathy and admiration to be inadequate. Miss Smyth-Bruce continued.

"An' hall I want is work," she said. "I'm a honest 'ardworking wo-lady, an' hall I want is work. An' is there work in the world for me?" She spread out her eloquent lace-decked arms again. "No!"

Felicity roused herself from the stupor into which Miss Smyth-Bruce's eloquence was throwing her. Now or never was the time to prove herself faithful to her principles.

"Come home with me, Miss Smyth-Bruce," she said earnestly. "I'm sure that we shall be able to find work for you."

Miss Smyth-Bruce blinked her bleary eyes. She looked a trifle disconcerted.

"W-work, dearie?" she said in a meditative voice. "I'm not strong, you know, dearie. I——"

"Oh, your legs, of course," said Felicity. "How are they?"

"They're so-so, dearie. Very so-so to-day, love."

"Well, come home with me, anyway," said Felicity. "You can rest them till they're better."

Miss Smyth-Bruce brightened. She glowed. She bridled.

"Oh, yes, rest, dearie," she said. "That will be very nice. Very nice indeed. I always say that anyone as is genteel needs plenty of rest. Don't you agree with me, dearie? Now low work doesn't suit me at all. Never did. Not since a child. But nice, refined work and not too much of it—well, that's walking down another pair o' shoes, as the poet ses, isn't it, love? I'm sure you agree with me. As you say, rest before heverything."

"Can you come home with me now?" said Felicity.

Miss Smyth-Bruce arose.

"Certainly, dearie," she said. "Excuse me one moment."

She vanished into an inner room and returned almost immediately. She wore an ancient, voluminous, black satin cloak, heavy with dusty and torn lace and ribbons. Her bonnet was indescribable. Suffice it to say that it was perched upon her wispy, untidy head, that it was a quivering nest of bedraggled black lace and faded imitation violets, that it was tied beneath her chin by two worn black ribbon strings. Her toilet was completed by a pair of black cotton gloves from which the ends of most of her fingers protruded unashamed. She went across to the filmy mirror on the overmantel and inspected her appearance. Evidently it pleased her. She turned to Felicity with a coy, radiant smile.

"Got any powder, dearie?" she said.

"No," said Felicity.

"Quite right, too," said Miss Smyth-Bruce approvingly. "When I was your age I never used powder. In fact, dearie, when I was your age we might have been twins. Not offended, love, are you?"

"No," said Felicity; "are you ready?"

During the journey Felicity's spirits sank lower and lower. No one could have accused Felicity of cowardice, yet the thought of the moment when she must introduce her strange companion at Bridgeways Hall sent little shivers up and down her spine. Of course, all Socialists had to go through this sort of thing, she supposed.

The discovery when they got out at the station that she had lost her purse depressed her still more.

Her purse was, as a matter of fact, at that moment reposing in one of Miss Smyth-Bruce's inner pockets. Miss Smyth-Bruce had been trying to abstract Felicity's purse from her bag since she met her and had at last managed it successfully in a tunnel.

"Now," she said in a tone of dismay, when Felicity told her of its loss, "you don't say so, dearie! Well, it never pours but it rains, doesn't it? It's probably in the train. You write to Scotland Yard, love, and you'll get it back. There's a silver cloud to every lining, don't forget, dearie. Now which is the way home, love? No conveyance to meet us? Never mind, love, I'm used to roughin' it, Hi am!"

With a light, free step, her head held high, her blue eyes full of courage and a sinking at her heart, Felicity led her protegee homewards.

They entered the hall under the shocked gaze of Moult. Moult's expression resembled that of a pious verger who has just seen the squire's lady eating an orange in church. Felicity had hoped to have a few words of explanation alone with her aunt before introducing Miss Smyth-Bruce. But the drawing-room door was open and her aunt came out into the hall at once. The light in the hall was very dim,

"Ah, Mary!" said Lady Montague. "Welcome from Russia, my dear!"

Felicity had completely forgotten the cousin from Russia. She remembered her now with a start. She opened her mouth to correct the error, then closed it again. The mistake was at any rate a welcome respite.

"Pronounced Marree, dear," said Miss Smyth-Bruce, following Lady Montague from the dim hall into the full light of day in the drawing-room. There was a gasp of horror in the drawing-room as the full light of day fell upon Miss Smyth-Bruce. Lady Montague blenched and closed her eyes. Miss Smyth-Bruce was not disconcerted.

"Pronounced Marree," she repeated, smiling graciously upon the assembled company, then raising on high the black cotton gloved hand, she greeted Lady Montague with ultra-refined accents. "Haw do you do? So pleased to meet you!"

Felicity stood in the doorway, looking round the room. Her grandfather had come downstairs. He was sitting in an armchair by the fireplace, his gouty foot encased in bandages and raised on to a padded pouffe. His face went purple and the look of an enraged bull came into it as Miss Smyth-Bruce entered. The bishop was standing in front of the fireplace holding a cup and saucer in one hand and a cake in the other as he talked gravely to Rosemary. His mouth fell open and his nerveless hand let his cake drop upon the hearthrug as his gaze met Miss Smythe-Bruce. Lady Montague opened her eyes. It was still there. She closed them again and opened them again. It was still there. This horror was still there. And it was real. And it was Cousin Mary from Russia who had come on a visit of indefinite length. Lady Montague's face was the face of one who has received a shattering shock and finds to her surprise that she is still alive.

Miss Smyth-Bruce sat down and began to draw off the black cotton gloves, holding them almost at arm's length with the air of a battered duchess.

"Mary." So they knew her and were expecting her. This family evidently meant to adopt her. She'd heard of such people—cranks, loonies, like this, but never had the luck to meet them before. She'd make the most of it, anyway. Her eyes roved round the room in search of small and easily removable valuables.

The bishop was the first to recover. With a resource and self-possession worthy of a higher cause he turned politely to Miss Smyth-Bruce.

"You—you're from Russia, Miss—er—er—um?" he

*

Lady Montague was still too overcome to perform any introductions.

Russia. Miss Smyth-Bruce carried on a large business in begging letters, and considering that she had to pay the first floor back what she considered quite an extortionate sum for writing them (her own handwriting and orthography being of the more rudimentary type) she made a fair profit. She remembered vaguely that she had written one pathetic letter in the character of a Russian refugee. This must be the one. She sometimes got rather confused about her letters. Still, this was evidently the Russian one—it had fairly "clicked," too.

She turned the full force of her devastating smile upon the bishop, and the bishop blenched.

"Yes," she said elegantly. "Russia! An' you've no idea, believe me, your grace, 'ere in peaceful Hengland, of them there Russians. Thieves an' scoundrels, one an' all, your reverence. As the Bible says, 'all that is gold does not glitter'—believe me."

Lady Montague was past coming to anyone's help. She had sent Moult for her smelling salts, and she was lying back in her chair, her eyes fixed with fearful fascination upon Miss Smyth-Bruce. A shade of black was beginning to mingle with the purple on Sir Digby's countenance. His first stupor was past. Rosemary remained frigidly aloof. Felicity sat demurely on a chair by the door. She had decided to let the situation take its course.

The bishop alone rose to the occasion.

"You met with—er—discomfort, I take it," he said, "at the hands of the Bolshevists?"

Miss Smyth-Bruce had just taken a sandwich from the cake-stand which stood beside her. She held it up daintily between thumb and first finger with all the other fingers cocked to their utmost capacity and turned to the bishop.

"You're right, your grace," she said, and the dusty lace and violets of her bonnet quivered emphatically as she spoke. "I should say I did! Stripped me of practically he very thing except what I stand up in, rejewced me to habject poverty, and a nervous wreck. But a nice rest, a nice long rest'll set me up fine!" She looked round the room and then turned to Lady Montague. "Classy little place you've got heaar," she said.

Lady Montague said nothing. She was dumb and paralysed with horror.

Miss Smyth-Bruce turned to Sir Digby and looked him up and down from his furious face to his invalid foot. Then she turned again to Lady Montague.

"Hubby hurt 'is foot?" she said. "Well, he has my sympathy, poor man. I know what it is. Tramping through Russia didn't do my poor feet any good, either. Believe me."

This was more than Sir Digby could stand.

He began to sputter furiously, his face a dull magenta.

Felicity thought then that there must come an explosion from Sir Digby that would wreck the universe. But instead came a diversion.

The door opened and a man in policeman's uniform appeared. Now, Miss Smyth-Bruce's past held sundry episodes that made the appearance of a man in policeman's uniform unwelcome.

There came the startling vision of Miss Smyth-Bruce in all her rusty draperies flying across the room, leaping with amazing agility over the low window-sill and scuttling down the drive.

Lady Montague was too stupefied even to ask for the smelling salts.

The policeman advanced. It was Ronald. He held the door open for a handsome, fashionably-dressed woman who followed him.

"It's Cousin Mary," he said. "She missed the train she asked you to meet so rang me up to run her down here. Excuse my costume, but I'm going on to dinner with the Burtons and a fancy dress dance. I make rather a nice bobby, don't I? I came down in an overcoat with my helmet in the dicky, so as not to make the Force jealous. Cousin Mary, this is everyone—Aunt Marcella, Rosemary, Felicity, grandfather. But, I say, who was your friend—the one who jumped out of the window?"

Lady Montague was recovering. She had begun to recover as soon as the figure of Miss Smyth-Bruce had disappeared from view.

She sat up very straight, blinked several times, then turned a cold, stern eye upon Felicity.

"Perhaps you have something to say about this, Felicity?" she said grimly.

Felicity looked from one to the other.

Lady Montague's face registered stern accusation, Sir Digby's fury to the verge of apoplexy, the bishop's pained resignation, Ronald's amusement, and Cousin Mary's surprise. And they were all looking at her in silence waiting for her to speak.

"Yes," said Felicity, "I'm on the horns of a dilemma. I mean I'm not a Socialist any longer. I mean, she couldn't have had chronic legs, could she?"

Then vivid memories of the past ten minutes overcame her, and burying her face in her handkerchief she fled from the room.

Chapter Four

Felicity Joins "The Oranges"

"Ronald's here," said Felicity.

"I know," said Franklin. "Don't sit on the desk, there's a good girl. You always sit on the papers I want most, and then I'm held up till you choose to get off."

Felicity grinned with sixteen-year-old impudence and sat upon a large corner of the knee-hole desk, swinging slim, gleaming legs.

"That's why I do it," she said. "You can't attend to me properly with half your brains scribbling notes on nasty bits of paper. How do you know that Ronald's here? Have you seen him?"

"No," said Franklin. "I've heard him. Or, rather, I haven't heard him—I've heard Sir Digby."

"Where?"

"Upstairs."

"Oh, yes—it's a bad day, isn't it? An upstairs day. Is he very—gouty? Gouty is a euph—whatever you call it."

"Euphemism, you mean, Pins."

"Yes, Frankie. You're awfully cultured. Fancy knowing words like that. Without a dictionary, too. Well, to return to my nicest and only unmarried brother—what exactly did you hear?"

"I heard Sir Digby speaking to him."

"Not speaking, Frankie," said Felicity reprovingly—"not speaking. Don't let your respect for grandfather run away with your sense of truth. You may have heard him roaring. Or bellowing. But not speaking. He doesn't speak on his bad days. Oh, here is Ronald."

A tall, pleasant-looking and very handsome young man entered.

"Hallo, Franklin," he said, shaking hands with the secretary, and then: "Hallo, Pins," pulling her pigtail.

He sat down on the desk beside her with a hand on her shoulder.

"You've been getting into trouble, Ron," said Felicity, with mock sternness. "Frankie heard."

Ronald grinned.

"I should think he did," he said. "I should think everyone from here to London heard. I have rotten luck. I can come down here for no particular reason and find the old boy quite jovial, but if ever I come down in a hole and wanting a little grandfatherly pecuniary assistance, I always hit on him in a foul temper."

"Gout, dear," said Felicity. "We always call it gout. It sounds better. Nobody's quite sure which is the cause and which is the effect—but the result is the same. What have you been doing, Ron—drinking or betting?"

"Neither, you impertinent young hussy. I was idiot enough to back a bill for another idiot and I've got let in."

"How much?"

"Four hundred quid."

"*Ron!*" said Felicity. "Frankie, listen to that! Have you got four hundred quid to lend us? We'll pay you when we get our next Saturday pennies."

"I haven't," said Franklin, "or you could have it with pleasure."

"He's longing to get on with his work, Ron," said Felicity, "and I'm sitting on all this morning's correspondence. He's trying to be patient, but he'll get an attack of gout if we stay much longer. Let's leave him to his nasty bills and love-letters. Let's go and find the dogs."

She went out whistling. Ronald stayed for a few minutes talking to Franklin, then followed her. They walked through the open front door into the sunny drive.

"Nice chap, Franklin," said Ronald.

"He's an absolute duck," said Felicity. "I don't know what I'd do without him. He's a sort of anti-whatever-you-call-it to grandfather and Aunt Marcella. I should turn into a stone-dead mummy in a day if I were left quite alone with them. But, Ron darling, what about you? What are you going to do about the money?"

He shrugged and laughed.

"Oh, don't worry about that," he said. "I shall manage somehow."

"You won't try grandfather again?"

"Good lord, no."

She glanced at him quickly. She read anxiety beneath his light manner.

"Don't you worry your old red head over that," he said again, pulling her thick copper plait affectionately.

They had reached the stable now and the dogs sprang out at them in welcome. Then they walked through the woods and up the hill. Ronald did not refer to the money again. He was the most charming of companions, and he liked Felicity. He refused to stay for lunch, and Felicity went down to the station with him to see him off. As he said good-bye he slipped a pound note into her hand.

"Sorry it can't be more this time, kid," he said, "but times is 'ard."

As the train moved off he leant out of the carriage and waved a smiling "good-bye" to her.

She walked away very slowly, holding her pound note in her hand.

Felicity had worshipped Ronald from childhood.

She went to the library again, where Franklin was still busy at the desk.

She took out her pound note and held it meditatively.

"Frankie," she said, "do you know of any way of turning one pound into four hundred?"

"No, my child," he said, "or I shouldn't be here."

"Of course, there's betting," she said; "but you never can be absolutely certain which horse is going to win."

"That is the drawback to betting," agreed Franklin drily. "I've often found that."

"Isn't there *any* way one could make four hundred pounds in a day or in a week?"

"There's the stage," said Franklin.

"The stage!" cried Felicity. "Now why didn't I think of that before? How does one get on the stage, Frankie?"

"Devious ways," said Franklin. "Some are born to the stage, some attain the stage, and some have the stage thrust upon them."

"Thrust upon one sounds the best way—the least trouble, I mean. What do you do to have it thrust upon you, Frankie?"

"Well, you can make a hit in an amateur show or a concert party somewhere and London's greatest manager—who has been listening and watching incog, at the back with rapture and amazement—comes up to you at the end with tears streaming down his cheeks, clasps your hand, and says: 'My boy—or my girl, as the case may be—will you join us at the Hipposeum at a thousand pounds a day. This paltry sum is just to start on. We will, of course, increase your salary materially after the first week or so.'"

Felicity drew a deep breath.

"It *does* sound nice," she said. "Do you happen to know of any amateur show in need of a heroine?"

"No," said Franklin, "I don't. You see, it's the heroine who always gets them up. She collects a little committee and says: 'Let's act a play. Now who's to be the heroine? I can't think of anyone to be heroine—of course, I couldn't do it.' Then the committee says: 'Of course you can, dear. You're just the person.' So it's all fixed up."

"You've a nasty cynical mind, Frankie," said Felicity. "I've suspected it for some time. But the stage is quite an idea. Thank you so much for suggesting it. Goodbye."

She went up to her bedroom, struck a tragic attitude before her looking-glass, and said in a sepulchral voice:

"'Is this a dagger that I see before me?

"'The handle towards my hand? Come, let me clutch it.

"'I have——'"

She took a quick, stealthy step forward in the manner of the old tragedians and fell over a small footstool. She picked herself up and rubbed her shins. Then she flung her long gleaming plait over her shoulders and struck a fresh attitude.

57

"To be or not to be, that is the question."

She looked around furtively, stepped backwards and fell over a small chair. She picked herself up again and rubbed her shins again.

"Not Shakespeare, I think," she remarked rather severely to her dressing-table. "I don't think Shakespeare's going to be lucky for me."

Then she flitted down the back stairs to Mrs. French's room.

"Good-morning, dearie," she said.

"Good-morning," said Felicity, sitting down upon a small footstool by the window. "Doesn't the half-hour before lunch when you're really hungry seem to last for hours and *hours*?"

Mrs. French went to a cupboard. From the cupboard she brought out a large tin. Felicity had known that tin from childhood. She clasped her knees hard with both arms and screwed up her face.

"Oh, scrummy," she said—"brandy snaps!"

Still beaming, Mrs. French put the tin on the floor by Felicity.

"There, dearie," she said.

Felicity began to nibble brandy snaps with small, white teeth. Felicity was still at the age when a morning's reckless consumption of cakes does not in any way impair one's appetite for lunch.

"I'm going on the stage, Mrs. French," said Felicity cheerfully.

"Well, I never, dearie," said Mrs. French, still beaming.

"Just till I've made four hundred pounds," said Felicity. "I shall probably come off the stage then."

"Well, I never did," said Mrs. French again.

"Tragedy, I think," went on Felicity; "but not Shakespeare. Something like this."

She leapt up from her footstool and struck another attitude.

"A-ha! Villain, wouldst thou?" she said through her teeth, addressing the footstool from which she had arisen, "I hate thee, I spurn thee! F-hare well!"

She flung herself tragically from the room, colliding violently with Moult, the butler, who was carrying a loaded tray past the door. Moult and the tray sat down and Felicity, with a look of horror and a murmured apology, fled. Her last vision was of Moult sitting motionless in a ruin of broken crockery and looking after her reproachfully.

She and Franklin had lunch alone.

"Comedy, I think it will be," she said to Franklin— "not tragedy."

"I've heard," said Franklin, "that tragedy is much easier."

"It may be," said Felicity, "but things get in your way so."

Lady Montague, Felicity's aunt, did not officially live at the Hall, but she spent a good deal of her time there. When she was not actually staying at the Hall she lived at the Dower House at the end of the park, which, from Felicity's point of view, was almost as bad. At this time, however, much to Felicity's relief, she was staying with friends in Scotland. Before she went she had arranged Felicity's time-table. She had arranged for the French master to come on Monday, the Italian master on Tuesday, the music master on Wednesday, and the singing master on Thursday, and for Felicity to go up to town to a dancing lesson with her maid on Friday. She said that Felicity must give Saturday entirely to music practising and foreign languages, except perhaps for a short drive with her grandfather. Needless to say, Felicity did none of these things. To-day was Thursday. Directly after lunch she went to the telephone.

"Please tell Mr. Sladyn," she said in her aunt's best manner, "that Miss Felicity Harborough will be unable to have her lesson this afternoon." Then she hung up the receiver, whistling gaily to herself.

Half an hour later, accompanied by an Irish terrier, a Great Dane, and a Sealyham, she was swinging blithely across the park. At the end of the park she vaulted lightly over the low wall into the road and swung on, still whistling.

Then she stopped. A motor-car stood by the roadside, and by it stood a tall, lugubrious-looking man. A fluffy, fair-haired girl sat near him on a suit-case, and another man was evidently beneath the car. All that could be seen of him was a stout pair of boots. Tinker, the Irish terrier, didn't like the boots, and fell upon them with growling fury. Felicity called him off and apologised.

"I'm so sorry," she said, holding him by the collar. "He's all right, really. He just doesn't like boots when he can't see the rest of the person."

The rest of the person slowly extricated itself from beneath the car and brought to light a short, stout man, with a round and cheerful countenance freely bedewed with mingled perspiration and oil.

"He won't mind you now," said Felicity. "Has something gone wrong?"

The short, fat man grinned, and the tall, thin one groaned, simultaneously.

"It's our unlucky day," said the fat man. "Everything that could go wrong is going wrong or has gone wrong."

Felicity nodded wisely.

"I know that sort of day," she said. "Buttons come off and you're late for breakfast and you spill coffee on to your best dress, and everyone else seems in a beastly temper all the time."

"That's it," said the fat man. "You've hit it. We've had that sort of trouble, but worse, ever since we got up."

Felicity sat on the running-board of the car, her head cupped in her hands, her auburn plait over her shoulder.

"Do tell me your troubles," she said, "I love hearing about people's troubles!"

"Well," said the fat man, "I'll introduce us first. I'm Percy, and he," pointing to the thin man, "is Freddy, and she," pointing to the girl, "is Peggy."

"Just Christian names?" said Felicity. "How nice!"

"We haven't any surnames," said the fat man solemnly. "We're 'The Oranges,' a concert party at Westsea, and we perform on the front every afternoon at three o'clock prompt, wet or fine. There are only the four of us."

"Four of you," said Felicity slowly, looking round. "Where's the fourth?"

"Ah," said the fat man, "that's one of the troubles!" The thin man groaned again. "The fourth is Rosie, and we went to give a show at Frean last night, and this morning Rosie has a headache."

"Not what you think," said the thin man dismally. "She only had stone ginger for dinner and she went to bed directly after the show."

"I didn't think anything," said Felicity with spirit.

"Anyway," said the fat man, "Rosie's headache is so bad that she couldn't come back to Westsea with us, and we haven't been able to get anyone to take her place, and—and it'll be a wash-out. You see, Peggy's voice is a contralto and Rosie's is a soprano, so Peggy can't take on her things. And who ever heard of a concert party of only three? Four is rather select and chic, but three—three's ludicrous! Peggy found a pal who'd do it—but, oh my, such a fright! One sight of her face would have emptied the beach! You see, it's got to be voice *and* appearance."

"W-would I do?" said Felicity rather anxiously. "Would you take me?"

The fat man looked at her.

"You—you don't mean it?" he said. "You aren't serious?"

"Oh, yes, I am," said Felicity. "I'm looking for an opening on the stage, and I think this would do very well as a beginning."

The fat man was still looking at her.

"Can you sing?" he said.

"I've just begun to learn—soprano," said Felicity.

"Can you dance?"

"More or less," said Felicity. "I can soon pick anything up."

"B-but what about your people? Would they let you?"

"I'm my own mistress," said Felicity very haughtily.

The tall, thin man broke in excitedly.

"Stop arguing!" he said. "Show her the things. She—she's wonderful. She—she'll make the show, I tell you. What do you say, Peggy?"

Peggy looked Felicity up and down.

"She's a peach," she said slowly, "but—oh lord, look at her hair and think of the colour of our togs! It'll kill them stone dead!"

Consternation came into all faces.

"What's the matter?" said Felicity, aghast.

"Our costumes," said the fat man, "are orange slightly diluted by the strong rays of the summer sun. Peggy's right. Your hair would kill them stone dead. It would show them up for the faded rags they are. Rosie is dark." Felicity stared in front of her in dismay, then with a little scream of excitement took out Ronald's pound note. "Could I hire a black wig with this?" she said.

The fat man turned head over heels in the road. He returned to normal position with a coating of dust dimming his coating of perspiration and oil, but by no means dimming the radiance of his smile.

"She's got a brain! She's got a brain!" he chanted. "Just the thing! We'll get one in Westsea. I don't know your name, Miss—er—um—but you'll have to be Rosie. The public of Westsea is used to Rosie. When can you be ready?"

Felicity pulled off Tinker, who was worrying the fat man's boots again. The Great Dane was sitting serenely by Peggy and the Sealyham was hunting for rabbits in the ditch.

"Now. Any time. I'll take the dogs to the corner of the road and send them home. I won't be a minute."

"Right, Rosie. We'll be getting out the things you'll want and then we'll run through the show with you." Felicity returned dogless in a few minutes. Peggy was just taking from a small case an orange-coloured pierrette dress with black ruff and belt. She held it against Felicity.

"Just right," she said. "Might have been made for you. When we get your black wig you'll look a treat . . . Now about the songs."

She sat down on the running-board beside Felicity and took some songs out of a case. The thin man sat down on the roadside and stared lugubriously at Felicity. The fat man disappeared beneath the car again. Felicity hummed the songs over. She soon picked up tunes and words. "Smile here . . . sigh here" . . . commanded Peggy.

"You'd better do them just as Rosie does them. The public expects it."

Finally Felicity stood up and sang one through, smiles, sighs, and all. Felicity had a very sweet, clear voice.

"By Jove!" said the thin man, overcome by his emotion. "By—by Jove!"

"Rather sloppy affairs, aren't they?" said Felicity.

"They're what the public likes," said Peggy. "Now for the dance. You only do one. With me."

Felicity was as light as thistledown and as graceful as a silver birch. In five minutes she had picked up the dance. The fat man, who had come from under the motor-car with another coating of oil and perspiration, turned head over heels again with delight, and acquired yet another coating of dust.

"Well," he said, "there's just time to get to Westsea and get the wig before the show begins."

"Will the car go?" said Peggy.

"How can I tell till I've tried?" said the fat man.

He got into the steering seat and drove the car forward for two yards, then stopped it.

"Yes, it goes," he said. "Pack in."

"What was wrong with it?" said the thin man mournfully. "What did you do to it?"

"I don't know," said the fat man cheerfully. "I never know. I just take things out and put them back and sometimes it makes it go and sometimes it doesn't. Ready, Rosie?"

"The Oranges" concert had begun and both the enclosure of chairs in front of them and the beach in the immediate vicinity were crowded. Regular patrons had already discovered the fact that there was a "new Rosie" and were excitedly approving of her. Felicity had had some difficulty with the black curly wig, but had at last managed to put it over her own wealth of bundled hair. An orange bandeau successfully concealed the joinings.

Percy was excruciatingly funny and Freddy sang mournful songs about the cruel sea and his broken heart in a dismal baritone. Peggy sang old favourites such as "Killarney" and "Annie Laurie," and had a bright little comic scene with the irrepressible Percy. And Felicity was Rosie. She was Rosie without a hint of self-consciousness and her "turns" were received with rapturous applause.

There was a five minutes' interval in the middle, and just before it Felicity danced. She danced gracefully and prettily, yet a close observer might have detected a slight nervousness in her manner.

Such an observer also might have seen that at the beginning of the dance she seemed to notice with a start of horror a large, old-fashioned carriage which was coming slowly down the promenade. In the carriage was an elderly gentleman with a very red face, resting his foot on the opposite seat. The carriage slowed down near "The Oranges" stand and the elderly gentleman looked with casual interest at the concert party. Suddenly his attention seemed to be riveted on to one of them. He shouted at the footman seated on the box. He pointed with his stick at the concert party.

Felicity finished her dance and the five minutes' interval was announced. Freddy came up to her.

"It's too hot for you on the stage," he whispered with lugubrious solicitude. "I've put a deck-chair for you down on the sand in the shadow of the stand. It'll be cool and more restful for you. No one'll disturb you. But if they do—if any blighter starts getting fresh with you—you just call 'Freddie' and I'll come and push his face in. I'll be just on the stand."

Felicity went down to the deck-chair he pointed out. But already there was some commotion in the waiting crowd. The elderly, red-faced man was pushing his way through it, uttering snorts of fury and brandishing his stick. He came up to Felicity.

"You little devil!" he stormed, "How dare you!"

Felicity looked him haughtily up and down. She showed no emotion at all except indignation at being so addressed.

"Who are you?" she said.

He went purple.

"Who am I?" he said. "You little devil. You——"

Felicity put up a languid hand and arranged the black curls of her wig. The elderly gentleman looked at it and faltered. He hadn't noticed the black hair. He was rather short-sighted, and he'd thought it and the bandeau together formed a hat of some sort.

His mouth dropped open. His fury died away, then gathered force again. As if he didn't know the little devil's face, every line of it—hair or no hair.

"You'll come straight home with me now——" he shouted in a tearing rage.

Felicity had found in the pocket of Rosie's dress a tiny powder-box and puff. Felicity now held it at arm's length and powdered her perfect nose. No one watching her would have thought that it was the first time Felicity had ever performed the operation.

"Freddie!" she called as she did so.

Freddie at once appeared.

"This man," said Felicity, pointing to her enraged grandfather, "is getting fresh with me. Please send him away."

Now Freddie was not a brave man, but the first sight of Felicity had bowled him over, and the courage of a man in love defending his beloved is proverbial. He advanced upon the purple-faced Sir Digby. "Do you want your face pushed in, sir?" he shouted. "Take yourself off or I'll call the police!"

Sir Digby emitted a frenzied bellow of rage and lifted his stick. The footman had seen the disturbance and was hurrying down to him. The crowd were murmuring hostilely against him. Felicity was still calmly powdering her nose. She'd always wanted to know what it was like. She found it rather tickly.

The footman had seized the stick and was persuading Sir Digby to go back to the carriage. He said he'd only make his foot worse if he didn't. And Sir Digby, looking furtively at the apparently unselfconscious dark-haired maiden powdering her nose, began to think that perhaps he'd made a fool of himself, and went away with the footman, telling the footman as he went as to what he thought of him. The footman was used to Sir Digby's bad days and didn't mind.

The bell rang for the second part of the programme. Rosie took her place on the platform.

"What was all the fuss about?" said a young man in the front row to his neighbour.

"Some old blighter insultin' of Rosie," said the neighbour. "Ought to be ashamed of himself at his age."

Felicity, looking very demure in the plainest of white crepe-de-Chine dresses, her red plait hanging down her back, dined with her grandfather and his secretary. Sir Digby was watching her closely.

Of course, he'd not been mistaken. Hair or no hair, he'd not been mistaken. The little *devil* . . . "This man's getting——" The little devil . . . He began to breathe hard and quickly.

"I'm glad to see you down, grandfather dear," said Felicity pleasantly.

"You didn't know I was down before, did you?" he growled.

She looked at him in innocent amazement.

"How should I?" she said. "You were in your room at lunch. Frankie and I had it alone."

He growled again.

"And where have you been this afternoon?" he said, his eyes fixed upon her narrowly.

She put some salt in her soup very daintily.

"I?" she said. "Oh, to-day's my singing lesson day . . . And where have you been, grandfather dear?"

"To Westsea," he exploded.

"Was it nice?" she said carelessly.

"Never been there, have you?" he growled.

"Oh, yes," she said, "lots of times. But I meant—was it nice to-day?"

He subsided into partial silence, only growling ferociously at intervals. Felicity kept up a pleasant conversation with Franklin rather in the manner of a Society hostess. Franklin was thoroughly mystified. But, as Felicity well knew, the worst was not over. Her grandfather called her into the library after the meal.

"Shut the door!" he bellowed. Felicity shut the door.

"Now," he thundered, "you little minx! You little devil! Deny it if you dare! You wore a black wig to deceive me, but——"

"I didn't wear a black wig to deceive you," said Felicity calmly. "I wore a black wig because my own hair clashed with the costume."

He gave a bellow of rage, but it changed abruptly into a chuckle . . . Felicity powdering her nose . . . Felicity calmly ordering that man to send him off . . . Felicity . . . the little devil . . . He'd secretly admired Felicity ever since, quite early in her childhood, he'd discovered that it was impossible to brow-beat her.

"Why did you do it, you monkey?" he said.

"I don't see why I should tell you," said his granddaughter.

"I'll give you ten pounds if you'll tell me."

Felicity considered this offer in silence. Then she said, "If you'll give me four hundred pounds, I'll tell you."

She thought for the minute that he was going to have apoplexy. He went purple and breathed like a bull. But he suddenly did the most eccentric thing he'd ever done in his life. He went over to his desk and wrote her a cheque for four hundred pounds. She folded it up and put it into her purse.

She went to the door, opened it, and turned back to look at him.

"I wanted to make four hundred pounds for Ronald," she said. "I only made four-and-six, but it's all right now."

Then she fled.

There pursued her down the corridor a furious bellow of rage that changed midway into a chuckle.

Chapter Five

Fate and Emerson Smith

Probably, if Lady Montague had been at home, Felicity would never have been allowed to visit Fairyng at all, because there was not the slightest doubt that Mr. Bennet, of Fairyng, was Sausages. One might have forgiven him for being Tea or Soap or even Boot Blacking. But not Sausages. Moreover, the placard, by means of which Mr. Bennet advertised his wares throughout the length and breadth of England, was almost as low as the wares it advertised. The placard represented the upper portion of an enormous man, red-cheeked, red-nosed, wearing a table napkin tucked in at the base of his innumerable chins and a large, fat, anticipatory smile, and holding on a fork, in a podgy hand, half-way to his mouth a large piece of sausage. This work of art bore the legend "HE LIKES THEM AND SO WOULD YOU." But one must be just. There were extenuating circumstances in the case. Mr. Bennet, at the outset of his career, had reluctantly decided not to give his own name to his sausages, because he didn't think that it went with them. There was nothing arresting about "Bennet's Sausages," so he called them "Aladdin's Sausages," and had a little picture on the label, of Aladdin in his cave standing, stupefied with amazement and delight, before a string of Mr. Bennet's sausages. So Mr. Bennet's name was not in anyway contaminated by the association . . .

It was this extenuating circumstance, and the fact that Mr. Bennet had married one of the Frymlons, of Frymlons (though she only lived a year after the marriage), that had induced Miss Barlow, of Minter House, Eastbourne, to admit Mr. Bennet's only child, Priscilla, into her select educational establishment, where she had met Felicity.

Fortunately, when the invitation arrived, Lady Montague was away paying a round of visits to her relations. Lady Montague paid a round of visits to her relations every year. She paid it in the spirit of a general inspecting his troops, and they received it in like spirit, holding their breath with apprehension and suspense, till she'd passed on, grim and majestic and disapproving, to the next victims. Lady Montague's round of visits, however, do not come into this story except to explain why Felicity was allowed to tarnish her social exclusiveness by a visit to Mr. Bennet's country seat, Fairyng.

The invitation was sent to Felicity's grandfather, Sir Digby Harborough, and Sir Digby happened to be in a good temper. A very good temper indeed. When the Bennet invitation arrived he hadn't had even a twinge of gout for over a week.

"D'you want to go?" he growled at Felicity.

Sir Digby always growled. You didn't tell whether he was in a good temper by whether he growled or not. You told by the note of his growl. This was quite a kind note.

"Oh, yes," said Felicity. "I'd love to."

"All right, then," growled Sir Digby. "Go . . . Go, then . . . Do you good—nice little change for you . . . and shut the door after you."

Sir Digby always dismissed people by telling them to shut the door after them . . .

A distant cousin of Mr. Bennet's wife, who kept home for him, received Felicity in the drawing-room. She wore a thick shawl on her shoulder and an over-fed Pom on her knee. She had a large pale face, rather like an under-done pancake, and small eyes like two currants.

"Dear child," she said, "I'm so glad to see you. Excuse my not getting up. I'm so *very* delicate. My chest, you know. Not to speak of my nerves. It's nothing but pure strength of will that keeps me alive. I don't eat enough to feed a bird. Pure strength of will and the love of my sweet little Popsy here . . ."

"Yap, yap!" said her sweet little Popsy with devastating shrillness.

"Priscilla?" said Felicity anxiously. Somehow she'd expected Priscilla to meet her at the station.

"Oh, my dear," said the lady, distressed, "*such* a worry. Poor Priscilla's sprained her ankle this morning. Nothing infectious or, of course, I wouldn't have let you come . . . and, of course, nothing serious. *Nothing* to what I have to put up with day in, day out. Young people like Priscilla simply don't know what real suffering means. . . . I suffer from *constant* ill-health. I eat hardly enough to keep a bird alive. . . . If it weren't for the constant love and sympathy of my little Popsy here——"

"Yap, *yap!*" said her little Popsy there.

"May I go up and see Priscilla?" said Felicity.

"Certainly, dear . . . Just touch that bell, will you, dear? I don't want to disturb dear Popsy by getting up, and sudden movements are so bad for the heart." A housemaid entered. "Take Miss Harborough up to Miss Priscilla's bedroom, please . . . You'll excuse me if you don't see me again till dinner time, won't you, dear? I need such a lot of rest. So does Popsy . . . we're both so delicate . . ."

Priscilla was sitting up in bed. Her pale face in its frame of dark curls was flushed, her eyes red-rimmed. Quite evidently Priscilla had been crying.

"Oh, Pins, darling," she said, "isn't it dreadful? I ought to have wired to you not to come, but I couldn't because I *did* want you so. I'm not really a bit bad, but I've got to stay in bed to-day. . . Oh, Pins, darling, it's so *lovely* to see you, but it'll be dull as ditch-water for you, and I *know* I oughtn't to have let you come."

Felicity threw her hat carelessly on to a chest of drawers and flung back her tawny plait. Her youth and confidence and health seemed to fill the room. She whisked across it and drew the half-closed curtain to its fullest extent. She switched on the electric light, then took the poker and dealt firmly and effectually with the smouldering fire. The light flooded the room. The fire blazed up. She turned the invalid's pillow, straightened her bed-clothes, and moistened her forehead with some eau-de-cologne which she found on the dressing-table.

"I *knew* everything would be different when you came," murmured Priscilla, nestling down in bed contentedly.

"Now I'm sure you're dying for tea," said Felicity briskly. "I am. Shall I ring, or does it come up by itself."

"It comes up or it doesn't," said Priscilla with a sigh. "I mean, they generally forget it—Cousin Sophia's too delicate to see to things much."

Felicity rang the bell. She gave her order to the housemaid with all the famous Harborough haughtiness. She was furious with all these people for neglecting Priscilla. The housemaid was impressed as never before had she been impressed since she entered the Bennet household. "My eye," she remarked in the servants' hall, "she's a one-er, she is. Looks an' all, she's got, too."

"Now," said Felicity, curling up in the armchair by the fire like the loose-limbed young animal she was, "who comes up here to look after you?"

"Well," said Priscilla after a slight pause, "Cousin Sophia's too delicate to stand the stairs, so she doesn't come. The maids bring up my meals . . ."

"What about your father?" said Felicity sternly. Priscilla flushed and turned away her face. Her underlip trembled slightly.

"Oh, Pins," she said, "I must tell you . . .You'd see for yourself,; anyway. Daddy's so *awfully* sweet, really, but—it began about a month ago . . . he's awfully *simple* and she's—she's a dreadful woman, but she flatters him and—you'll see her, she's staying here now . . . and oh, I'm *sure* she'll get him in the end . . . and I couldn't *bear* it. . . . People laugh at Daddy, but I know what a *dear* he is . . . but—but for this month he's not been like himself at all . . . she—she doesn't care *what* she does to get him . . ." Her voice died away.

Felicity uncurled, herself and sat up.

"Now you're just not to worry," she said firmly, "it's going to come all right."

"Is it, Pins?" said Priscilla eagerly, "how do you know?"

"I *know* it," said Felicity with conviction.

Priscilla lay back with a little sigh.

"I remember it used to be like this at school," she said dreamily. "Worries simply used to melt away when you came."

The housemaid entered with a tray of tea. She put it on the table by Felicity's chair.

Felicity put a slim hand on the teapot.

"The tea's half-cold," she said calmly, "and so is the toast. They're neither of them fit for an invalid. Please take them down and make some fresh."

The housemaid looked up pertly. When all was said and done, this was only a kid with her hair in a plait. Then she met Felicity's blue, blue eyes and the starch went out of her.

"Yes, miss," she said meekly.

Felicity went down the wide shallow staircase dressed for dinner. In the hall, by the fire, sat Cousin Sophia still wearing the shawl, and the Pom.

"You've been with Priscilla, dear?" she enquired, moving her chair farther away as Felicity approached. "How is dear Priscilla? I'd go up to see her if I could, but stairs are so bad for one's heart, and, after all, I have Popsy to consider. He's nervous and the atmosphere of a sick room upsets him . . ." A gong sounded discreetly and musically in the distance. "Ah, dinner," said Cousin Sophia, rising quite eagerly. "I always go in to meals, dear, and try to eat a little," she explained to Felicity, "because, of course, as I say, one must live, but, really, I hardly eat enough to keep body and soul together . . . Ah, here comes James!"

Mr. Bennet was descending the stairs. Mr. Bennet was for all the world like the advertisement of the sausages. He was almost as broad as he was long. His figure completely filled up the wide staircase as he descended. His chins resembled a range of innumerable mountains fading away into the distance. His face was red and round and smiling like an enormous baby's. He was almost bald, but upon one side of his head grew a little plantation of long, straggly grey hairs which he carefully brushed over the rest of his head, distributing them as impartially as possible.

He greeted Felicity.

"Priscilla's friend, ain't it?" he said. "Pleased to meet you, my dear . . . Hard lines on poor old Pris bein' laid up, ain't it? But we're *very* pleased to have you along with us, my dear, we are indeed. I used to hear a lot about you in the Minter House days . . . your games and pranks and what-not . . ." His eyes wandered restlessly to the staircase. "Mrs. Flower not come down yet, my dear?" he said to his cousin.

"No, James, I haven't seen her," said Cousin Sophia. "I haven't seen her since lunch, but I was lying down all the afternoon trying to get a wink of sleep . . . You know, I sleep so badly, dear," she said to Felicity, "I really hardly get enough sleep to keep body and soul together."

"Good evening, everybody," said a sprightly voice from the top of the stairs.

Mr. Bennet's red face flushed purple and a rather comical little love-lorn smile came to his lips.

A woman, handsome, stout, and well past her first youth, was coming downstairs. Her hair was of that vivid shade of gold with which Nature is less generous than art. It required little perception to see that Mrs. Flower owed hers to the more generous hand. She had applied black colouring matter to eyelashes and eyebrows with a lavishness worthy of a better cause. Neither face nor chest stood in need of colouring matter, but she had evidently attempted to tone down their vividness by a thick coating of white powder. She was dressed in a gown of silver tissue and had corseted her too, too-solid flesh so effectually that she looked as if she had been literally poured into her dress and, if there'd been one more drop, would have overflowed.

"Well,' she said, with a girlish little laugh, "there you all are! I do declare, Mr. Bennet, you do seem to get younger every day. Quite a boy you look from here!"

Mr. Bennet's smile grew more sheepishly delighted and his rubicund face grew more purple.

He introduced Felicity.

Mrs. Flower held out a red and massive arm with overelaborate politeness.

"*Sow* pleased to meet you," she said. "You will be nice company for poor Priscilla laid up as the pore child is. . . ." She turned her terrible roguish smile on to Mr. Bennet, then back to Felicity. "You'd never think he was the father of a grown-up daughter now, would you?" she said.

Felicity's clear, speedwell-blue eyes flitted from one to the other. "Why wouldn't you?" she said innocently at last.

Mrs. Flower looked taken back and Mr. Bennet's childlike smile faded.

"Let's go into dinner now," said Cousin Sophia plaintively. "I never feel quite safe in the hall with Popsy. It's so draughty . . . And I'm awfully worried to-day because I dreamed last night that he had a cold and I'm so afraid it may have been sent as a warning . . ."

"All right," said Mr. Bennet heartily, "let's go in to dinner."

"Not that I *want* to eat anything," said Cousin Sophia hastily, "I look upon eating simply as a *duty*."

Mrs. Flower talked a good deal during dinner. She was coy and roguish and merry and girlish. Mr. Bennet blushed and gazed at her incessantly. Felicity listened demurely, her eyes on her plate. Cousin Sophia was too busy eating and feeding Popsy, who sat on a high stool by her side, to have attention to spare for anything else. Cousin Sophia, if she looked upon eating as a duty, quite evidently was a living contradiction to the theory that senses of duty no longer exist. Cousin Sophia had a sense of duty that did her credit. Cousin Sophia, who had said she ate only enough to keep a bird alive, ate at that meal alone enough to kill whole aviaries full of birds. Felicity watched her with fascinated wonder . . .

Mrs. Flower was describing, evidently not for the first time, the more celebrated of her theatrical triumphs. Beneath her gush was a suspicion of deliberate care as if the pronunciation of some words and the aspiration of all aitches needed a certain amount of conscious attention.

"I was Juliet, then. . . . I just *adore* Shakespeare, don't you? . . . Oh, I *adore* him . . . there's better speeches in Shakespeare, I always say, than in any other plays goin' . . . but natchurally common people don't understand it . . . it takes people of education to understand Shakespeare . . . Now, as soon as I set eyes on Mr. Bennet here I said to myself, I said, 'Now *there's* a man that'll understand Shakespeare!'"

Mr. Bennet's sheepish grin dawned again upon his expansive rubicund countenance. But he was a truthful man and murmured: "I've never had no education. Not to speak of, that is."

This, however, did not disconcert Mrs. Flower.

"Perhaps not, Mr. Bennet," she said with a wave of a small fat hand. "Perhaps not . . . but there's some that is *born* with an education . . . a sort of *natural* education . . . Now the moment I set eyes on you I said to myself, '*There's* a man with a *natural* education.'"

"Just a *leetle* more chicken for Popsy," said Cousin Sophia to the waitress.

"You were telling us about you as Juliet," said Mr. Bennet with an admiring glance.

Mrs. Flower became coy.

"Well, I don't know as I *ought* to," she said, with a roguish little wriggle of her large body. "Really, I don't think I can *repeat* some of the things people said about me in the papers . . . you'd think— well, you'd think I was so conceited."

"No, we won't. I promise you," encouraged Mr. Bennet, "Do go on."

"No, I'll tell you what I'll do . . . I'll show you my press reports . . . mind you, though, as a show it was clean spoilt by Romeo. You've never seen such a stick as that man was . . . My goodness, he *was* a stick . . . Stick's hardly the word . . . Well, I told him what I thought of him afterwards . . . quite quiet and dignified I was about it, because I wouldn't demean myself by behaving any way but like a lady. Did he take it like a gentleman? Not a bit of it. He used language somethin' dreadful."

"Not *to you*?" said Mr. Bennet, looking quite ferocious

"Yes, to me . . . I was *that* upset, because I'm so sensitive. Would you think I was sensitive, Mr. Bennet?"

"Yes," said Mr. Bennet gallantly, "I would."

"Won't Popsy Wopsy finish up his gravy, den?" said Cousin Sophia.

"Of course I'm reserved," said Mrs. Flower, "and it's only those that know me really well that know how sensitive I am."

"I know," said Mr. Bennet.

The sparkling eyes were continually being rolled in his direction.

"Ah!" said Mrs. Flower with a deep sigh, "but you're so *sympathetic.*"

"Do you think I am?" said Mr. Bennet.

"*Wonderfully!*" said Mrs. Flower, clasping her hands. "*Running* over with sympathy, you are . . . I've never in all my life met such a personality . . . Such sympathy, imagination and—er—and sympathy. You know, you ought to have been an actor."

"Do you think so?" said Mr. Bennet in some surprise.

"Jus' anozzer 'ickle spoonful, darling," said Cousin Sophia, "to make Popsy a strong doggie."

"Oh, I do," said Mrs. Flower. "I *felt* it. I felt it as soon as I met you. The minute I set eyes on you I said to myself, '*There's* a man that ought to have been an, actor.'"

"Fancy that now!" said Mr. Bennet, impressed.

"I did indeed. I wouldn't say so if I hadn't. I've never told a lie in all my life. Not from the cradle. And now I've got to know you better I say it all the more. Your voice and—er—eyes and face, and all that. You were *born* to it. Have you never really acted?"

"Never," said Mr. Bennet.

Mrs. Flower raised her belladonna'd black-encircled eyes to the ceiling.

"One can hardly credit it," she said. "Here's a man formed by nature to be an actor, in face, voice, figure——"

Mr. Bennet pulled down his waistcoat and made an ineffectual effort to look slim, "and—er—all that, and— he's never acted." A look of purpose came into her face, "but," she went on, "you *must* act, Mr. Bennet. It's never too late to act . . . we must get up some theatricals now . . . here. . . . What about Macbeth?"

"Well, what about him?" said Mr. Bennet, gazing at her ardently.

Mrs. Flower's eyes dropped modestly before his ardour, then raised themselves . . .

"You see—you *are* Macbeth," she said dramatically, "the courage, the—the tempestuous impulsiveness, the —the heroic mould, they're all there. I knew they were. That was the first thing I thought about you. As soon as I set eyes on you I said to myself, '*There's* a man that ought to be Macbeth!'"

She paused for effect, one hand upraised.

"Ask anyone if I didn't," she added sententiously, somewhat spoiling her speech by this anti-climax.

"B-but I don't know anything about Macbeth," said Mr. Bennet. "I told you I'd never had no education to speak of. I learnt 'The Wreck of the Schooner Hesperus' at school, but that's all. I never learnt Macbeth."

Mrs. Flower made another dramatic gesture as though she had come to some momentous decision.

"I know," she said. "We'll do it. We'll get it up. We'll do it for the village. We'll arrange the scenes to-night. And you shall be Macbeth . . . Tell me," she leant forward to him earnestly, "has no one *really* ever told you that you ought to have been an actor?"

"No," said Mr. Bennet, evidently much impressed, "not till you did."

They went into the drawing-room after dinner. Mrs. Flower found a Shakespeare and sat down near—very near—Mr. Bennet on the sofa.

"The first thing to do," she said, "is to find a nice little scene and then to begin rehearsing. I simply *long* to see you as Macbeth . . . The courage—the tempestuous impulsiveness, the—the heroic mould . . . You," she raised her eyes beseechingly, "you *will* do it, won't you?—to please me."

Mr. Bennet gazed at her ecstatically. "Oh, yes," he said, "I don't say I'll be much good, but I'll do it," he gulped with emotion, "to please you."

A far-away look came into Mrs. Flower's eyes. She leant forward with a sudden jerk and fixed her eyes upon something invisible a few yards away that evidently roused in her deep emotion. She pointed a podgy forefinger at it. "Is this a dagger that I see before me?" she hissed dramatically.

Mr. Bennet followed the direction of her finger with open-mouthed amazement. "No," he said soothingly, "it's nothing to be frightened of. If you mean that thing on the mantelpiece, it's only a little silver thing they gave me when I laid the foundation of the Cottage Hospital. It's not a dagger."

"And what are you going to do now, dear?" said Cousin Sophia to Felicity.

"I'm going up to Priscilla if I may, please," said Felicity.

"Very nice, dear," said Cousin Sophia vaguely, "very nice indeed. And Popsy and I are going to our little refuge to rest. You'll come and see our little refuge, won't you?"

Felicity followed her across the hall and down a little passage to a room at the end. It was a very comfortable little room with a sofa, deep chairs and a blazing fire. A glass of hot milk and a plate of biscuits stood on a table by the chair. "This is where I rest," said Cousin Sophia, putting Popsy down upon a footstool in front of the fire. "I need such a lot of rest, dear, because I'm so delicate," she said as she sat down and began to sip the hot milk, "and I have to take extra nourishment between meals because I simply don't eat enough to keep a bird alive . . . Won't you sit down, dear? You can nurse my little Popsy if he'll let you. I'm sure you'd like that."

"Thank you so much," said Felicity, "but I think I'd rather go to Priscilla."

Priscilla was sitting up, her eyes fixed eagerly on the door.

"Oh, Pins, darling," she said, "I've been longing for you . . . Was everything *awful*?"

"Oh, no," said Felicity cheerfully. "Of course not. It was all quite jolly. Did they send you up a decent dinner?"

"Yes, piping hot. I think you scared them, Pins. I feel so ashamed of having let you in for all this. I know how awful Cousin Sophia is and—oh, that woman and—and you'll never guess how sweet Daddy really is."

Felicity was making up the fire, drawing the curtains and moving the armchair to Priscilla's bedside.

"Now let's be comfy," she said. Again confidence and youth and cheerfulness radiated from her, filling the room, putting to flight all the little demons that had been torturing Priscilla.

The next morning, at breakfast, Felicity gathered that, though the actual scene had not yet been chosen, the previous evening had not, from Mrs. Flower's point of view, been wasted. Her elderly admirer was more enamoured than ever. He blushed purple at her frequent glances and followed her about with his eyes and sighed heavily to himself at intervals.

"Is everything as you like it?" he said affectionately, watching her consume large quantities of eggs and sausages and bacon.

"Lovely," she said. She raised glowing eyes to his "How beautifully you look after one!" she said. "So—so *comforting* to one who's knocked about the world as I have."

There was a short silence.

"I know!" she said suddenly; "The Ghost Scene!"

"Eh?" said Mr. Bennet.

"The Ghost Scene."

"Who saw it?" said Mr. Bennet, mystified.

"Oh, you dear old stupid," laughed Mrs. Flower with her girlish tinkle, "I mean, we'll act the ghost scene from Macbeth. It's the very scene. I'm *magnificent* in the Ghost Scene." She pointed sternly at the coffee-pot. "'Stand not upon the order of your going, but go at once,'" she said in a sepulchral voice.

"Now don't start getting all excited," said Mr. Bennet soothingly, "you wear yourself out feeling things so."

"Well, I can't help my feeling nature," sighed Mrs. Flower. "Anyway, that's what we'll do. You Macbeth and me Lady Macbeth. There are some other people, but you can easily get one or two people from the village for that. And the ghost doesn't really matter, because he doesn't speak. Just anyone will do for the ghost."

She turned suddenly to Mr. Bennet and pointed a dramatic

forefinger at him. "Avaunt! and quit my sight! Let the earth hide thee!" she spat out venomously.

"Come, come now," said Mr. Bennet mildly, "that's a bit thick, that is."

"You say that to the ghost," said Mrs. Flower.

"Oh, do I?" said Mr. Bennet, relieved. "Seems asking for trouble, though, don't it? talking to ghosts in that tone of voice."

"Oh, I'm going to enjoy myself," said Mrs. Flower, "acting with a *real* actor at last." Breakfast was over. She rose from her seat, slipped her arm through his. "Come now, Macbeth, we're going to rehearse all morning."

She led him, his great face beaming like a child's with ecstatic pride and pleasure, into the library.

Cousin Sophia always spent the morning in bed resting and taking nourishment. The doctor came soon after breakfast and said that Priscilla might get up, but must spend the next few days in her room with her foot up.

"What's Daddy doing this morning?" said Priscilla, who looked very fragile as she sat propped up by cushions in the easy chair. Felicity was sitting cross-legged on the hearthrug.

"He's rehearsing Macbeth with Mrs. Flower," she said cheerfully.

"I've felt as if ten thousand weights had been lifted from me since you came," went on Priscilla, "but— you're *sure* it's going to be all right."

"*Sure*," said Felicity.

But she felt a good deal less sure than she pretended.

Preparations for the performance of Macbeth went on apace. Costumes were hired from London. Tickets were sold in the village. The Village Hall was engaged. The Vicar was asked to deliver an address on Shakespeare to introduce the scene. A few young men from the Young Men's Club were reluctantly persuaded to act as lords and murderers, and every morning, every afternoon, every evening, Mr. Bennet and Mrs. Flower rehearsed alone together in the library. The Young Men were supposed to rehearse by themselves Mrs. Flower said that they would be less nervous.

Then, on the morning of the actual performance, the bomb fell.

The engagement between Mr. Bennet and Mrs. Flower was announced. It was announced the morning after the final rehearsal in the library.

Coy and blooming and blushing and possessive was Mrs. Flower that morning.

Glum and silent and shrinking and wretched-looking was Mr. Bennet. His *debonair* assurance and lover-like radiance of the last few days had suddenly departed. But this did not seem to disconcert the lady. She had quite evidently consolidated her position and trusted to Time and her charm to win over her reluctant lover.

Of course the news could not be kept from Priscilla. Her little face paled. Her eyes grew tragic.

"Oh, *Felicity!*" she said. "You said——"

But Felicity's confidence still upheld her.

"My dear," she said with a look of deep wisdom upon her exquisite little face, "they're not married yet. There's many a slip, you know! You see, Priscilla, my idea is this. There's always a minute when you can *do* something if you're on the watch for it. It hasn't come yet, but— I'm on the watch for it all the time."

"What are they doing now?" said Priscilla.

"She's gone up to town to get the make-up for to-night and—I think he's in the library."

"Tell him to come up to me, will you?"

"Yes," said Felicity.

Mr. Bennet was in the library. He was sitting at his desk in an attitude of utter hopelessness with his bald head upon his large red hands.

"Priscilla wants you to go up to speak to her, please," said Felicity from the doorway.

"Oh, I can't," moaned Mr. Bennet. "I can't face the child after what I've done. Oh, why didn't you stop me? Why didn't somebody stop me? Why didn't *anybody* stop me? I never meant—I liked flirting with her and her making me think that I was—I was one of the lads and all that sort of thing . . . but I never meant— Look," he took a miniature out of his pocket and handed it to Felicity. It was a pale, sweet, oval face—a face like Priscilla's, with a frame

81

of dark curly hair, "that's my wife," he groaned, "that's Prissy's mother. . . . I shan't dare to meet her when—I tell you she's the only woman I've ever loved. And Prissy . . ."

"But why *did* you?" said Felicity rather sternly; "nobody made you."

"They did," said Mr. Bennet with spirit. "*She* did with her Macbeths and ghosts and things. Rehearsing all day long and one thing and another. I tell you I didn't know I'd done it till she told me I had, and she got a paper out for me to sign, and I signed it. Mind you, I was feeling fond of her at the time—last night that was— but when I woke up this morning I saw it all clear. I seemed to come to myself sudden-like. I'm what you'd call a downright common man myself, but my Helen was a lady and my Prissy's a lady an' *she*—she isn't—and this mornin' I saw it all clear. I've just let myself be flattered—you know, tryin' to pretend I was young and—and flighty, when I know really that I'm just a common old man, and that's how my Prissy likes me, and that's how I'm really content to be—but it's done now—it's too late . . . I've woke up in my right senses too late."

"Oh, nonsense," said Felicity.

No one could listen to the thrilling hope and encouragement of Felicity's voice and not take heart. He looked at her just as Priscilla had looked up at her . . .

"W-what do you mean?" he said.

Felicity laid a cool, slim hand for a second upon his great red one.

"It's going to be *quite* all right," she said in the tone in which a mother might comfort an unhappy child.

And, despite himself, something of his burden seemed to fall from him.

But Felicity was worried. And when Felicity was worried she always went for a long walk. So she went for a long walk this morning.

It was as she was coming back that she saw Mrs. Flower in the lane that led from the station, talking to a man.

He was a rather ornate sort of man with curling black moustaches and flashing diamond tiepin and rings, but in spite of this he had a nice face. They seemed to be arguing, he urging and she scornfully rejecting. Then she turned from him abruptly and walked away. When Felicity reached the spot where they had been talking, the man stood alone leaning against a gate and staring morosely in front of him.

"Good morning," said Felicity.

The man gave a start.

"Good morning, Miss," he said gloomily.

"Was that Mrs. Flower?" said Felicity innocently.

"Yes, Miss," said the man still more gloomily.

"I'm staying at Fairyng," went on Felicity, "and she'd gone into town to get some make-up for the theatricals. Do you know if she got it all right?"

"You stayin' at Fairyng?" said the man with sudden interest.

"Yes," said Felicity.

Then gloom fell upon him once more.

"She's going to marry 'im, isn't she?" he said, cocking a thumb vaguely in the direction of Fairyng.

"Well, they're engaged," said Felicity. "Don't you want them to be?"

"Me? Wants 'em to be?" said the man. He gave a short laugh. "That's a good 'un, that is! Me want 'em to be!" Then an admiration that was almost reverence crept into his voice. "But, I say, she's a beauty, ain't she? An' style. My word! . . . Now, wouldn't you take 'er for a duchess any day? She can put it on an' no mistake. Carry it orf with the Queen herself, she could."

"Are you in love with her?" said Felicity simply.

"Love with 'er?" said the man with another short laugh. "That's a good 'un, that is. Love with 'er? I've been in love with 'er hall me life. I used to go to 'er father's fish an' chip shop when I was a little nipper just for a sight of 'er. We went on the stage together, we did. Did turns together on the 'alls an' she'd of married me all right if——"

He paused.

"Yes?" said Felicity, "if——?"

"Hambition," said the man morosely. "Hambition, that was it. She wanted to be a lady. Always pickin' up little tricks, she was, till, has I said, you couldn't tell her from a duchess. So she married that there Flower chap wot run a travellin' Shakespeare show."

"Oh, yes, she's awfully fond of Shakespeare, isn't she?" said Felicity.

"Not she," said the man contemptuously, "got more sense, she 'as. Swank, that's what it is. *She's* one for the *'alls*, she is. She an' me together bring the 'ouse down. Why, 'er with 'er charm an 'er 'air an' er eyes—she's *myde* for the 'alls. *Shakespeare!* Bah!"

He spat the word out with withering contempt.

"Why did you come to see her to-day?" said Felicity, going daringly to the heart of the matter.

The ornate man did not resent her question.

"I've bin in' America this year doin' comic Music 'All turns an' I comes back 'ere to find old Flower dead meantime. Tyke it from me, she wasn't 'appy with 'im. She as good as told me so. 'Well,' I sez to myself, 'she'll 'ave learnt sense by this time, Hemerson Smith (Hemerson Smith's me name), an' you an she'll find 'appiness together.' So I tracks 'er down 'ere an' what do I find? She's got 'erself engaged to a pickled plutocrat wot keeps two cars and lives in one of the stately 'omes of England. Hambition, that's it. It'll be 'er downfall. She won't be appy with 'im. I told 'er so straight. 'Daisy,' I said, 'it's me what you loves and what you've always loved' (an she didn't deny it) 'an' if you let Hambition part us asunder agyne syme as what you did before, you'll regret to your dyin' day. 'For the last time,' I sez, 'will you marry me?' 'No,' she sez, quite firm, 'I'm doin' a good deal better for myself than *that*, Hemerson Smith.' 'All right,' I sez, 'it's the last time I asks you. I'm goin' to shoot myself an my ghost'll 'aunt you the rest of your life.' An she laughs in my fyce an' goes off," he ended gloomy.

"Are you going to shoot yourself?" said Felicity with interest.

"No," he said, "'corse I'm not. Mug's game, shootin' yourself. What's the matter, Miss?" he ended in surprise, for Felicity was standing with hands clasped, blue eyes alight and lips parted as if in ecstasy.

"It's the moment," she said, "I'm going to help you. Will you be at the Village Hall at quarter to eight, to-night?"

The Vicar's speech on Shakespeare was erudite, but above the heads of his present audience. The more intelligent of them gathered a vague impression that a man called Shakespeare had written a play called Bacon and had subsequently changed the title to Macbeth. The less intelligent gathered no impression at all. Cousin Sophia was not in the audience because Popsy had sneezed that afternoon, and Cousin Sophia, utterly prostrate, was awaiting the famous veterinary surgeon who had been summoned from London.

. . .

The curtain rose. The audience had been in doubt as to what kind of play this was going to be. But the appearance of Mr. Bennet as Macbeth left no doubt at all in their minds that it was going to be a rollicking comedy. They rocked with laughter. They applauded tumultuously. Their error was a pardonable one. None of the hired costumes fitted the actors anywhere at all. They were tight where they ought to have been loose and loose where they ought to have been tight. Mrs. Flower, of course, was magnificent. But she wasn't Lady Macbeth . . .

The comic effect of Mr. Bennet's costume was considerably heightened by his woebegone expression. He wore that look of wistful pathos that has made Charlie Chaplin immortal. The play began. Members of the Young Men's Club, inadequately garbed as Lords or Murderers, mumbled their lines inaudibly after the prompter . . .

The play dragged on.

Behind the scenes the Young Man who was to be the ghost, and so arrived after the others entered, was met at the door by Felicity. Felicity pressed a ten-shilling note into his hand.

"You won't be needed after all," she said sweetly. "Good-night."

The young man's spirits revived. He looked at the note to make sure it was real, then, lest someone should discover that it was a mistake and he was needed after all, vanished as hastily as he could into the night and, subsequently, into the White Lion.

A few minutes later Mr. Emerson Smith appeared. He looked about him suspiciously.

"'Ere I am, Miss," he said, "what's the gyme?"

But Felicity had no time for explanations.

"Take your hat off," she said quickly, "and stand still."

He took his hat off and stood still, and Felicity proceeded to wrap him round and round in endless folds of grey tulle.

"By Gum!" said Emerson Smith; then, feeling this inadequate, "Crikey!"

"Can you walk?" said Felicity.

"Just," said Emerson Smith after experiment.

Felicity opened the door that led on to the stage.

"May't please your Highness sit?" said one of the Lords impatiently when the prompter had repeated the sentence three times. The Lord was in real life the butcher's assistant and had been too busily engaged in trying to catch the eye of a lady friend in the back row to have much attention left for the prompter.

"Now just walk on and stand there and look at her," said Felicity, pushing Emerson Smith on to the stage.

Emerson Smith walked on and stood there and looked at her.

The dim lighting of the stage made the effect of Emerson Smith rather a good one. He looked more like a ghost than anyone who knew him would have believed possible. Lady Macbeth gazed at him and the colour slowly drained from her cheeks. Then, with a wild cry of "Help!" she fled from the stage. To the audience it was a fit and proper denouement to the scene. They enjoyed it more than they'd enjoyed any of it so far. They enjoyed it far more than they'd have enjoyed Shakespeare's own development of the situation. The curtain manipulators, after a minute's stupefaction, lowered the curtain.

Mr. Bennet sat down abruptly on the Queen Anne chair reserved for the ghost and wiped his brow.

Mrs. Flower fled down the road distraught.

"Oh, Em," she cried as she ran, "come back to me. I never thought you'd really go an' do it. Honest, I didn't. Oh, Em, I'll marry you if only you'll come back. . . . Oh, I never knew you'd really go an' do it . . ."

Behind her, still swathed in grey tulle and progressing by little leaps and bounds like a kangaroo, came Emerson Smith. Muffled cries of "Daisy!" proceeded from his ghost-like shroud. Mrs. Flower, out of breath (for there was little of the Atalanta in her physical composition), stopped at last and leant sobbing against a tree. Mr. Smith hopped up to her and, as well as he could, through his grey tulle, took her tenderly in his arms. She sobbed on his breast.

"Oh, Em," she said, "you don't feel a bit as if you was dead."

"I'm not," said Emerson Smith, releasing her and beginning to struggle like a captive fish with his all-enveloping net. "You will marry me, Daisy, now, won't you?"

"When I saw your ghost standing there, Em," said Mrs. Flower solemnly, "I knew I loved you, knew it too late. I said to myself, 'There, you've let the best man in the world go to his death for you and you'll never know a day's happiness the rest of your life.' I said that to myself, Em. I looked at the poor fish I'd said I'd marry and I thought to myself, 'What's wealth beside love? An' I've let him go an' kill hisself.' Oh, but I wouldn't 'ave married him *never* then. I'd sooner've gone into a monastery."

"They wouldn't've let you, Daisy," said Emerson, still floundering, and added, "Damn the stuff!"

Then Felicity arrived. She carried Mrs. Flower's cloak and without a word spread it over that lady's voluminous shoulders. Then she turned and helped to unwind Emerson.

Mrs. Flower looked at her in some surprise.

"Hello!" she said. "You're the kid that was staying at Fairyng, ain't you? Well," she thrust a hand into her bosom, brought out a piece of paper and tore it into shreds dramatically, "tell that old fish that I wouldn't marry him if he was the last man in the world . . . I'll send you a postcard where to send my things, and," she linked her arm through Emerson Smith's, "come on, old Em," she said affectionately, "let's go to your mother's to-night and get married first thing to-morrow morning. I'm through with ambition, I am. Let 'im keep 'is money, sausages an' all."

The three of them were in Priscilla's bedroom. Mr. Bennet sat by the couch and held his daughter's hand affectionately. He looked chastened but happy. Felicity was curled up in the armchair by the fire.

"As soon as you can travel, love," said Mr. Bennet to his daughter, "we'll go right away. Take a real holiday—just you an' me together. I feel as if I'd a lot to make up to you for," he added humbly. "I've been a very foolish old man."

"I'm going to bed," announced Felicity sleepily, "I'm awfully tired and I've got to go home to-morrow."

Priscilla turned shining eyes upon her.

"Oh, Felicity," she said, "if it hadn't been for you——!"

Felicity stretched her shapely young body.

"It wasn't I," she said, "it was just Fate—Fate and Emerson Smith!"

Chapter Six

Felicity and the Little Blind God

The train slid into the little country station and Felicity leapt down upon the platform with all the agility of her sixteen years.

She stood and looked about her, cheeks aglow, blue eyes alight. It was nice to be home again. She'd seen Mr. Bennet and Priscilla off that morning. They were going to Italy. Both were very happy. Then she'd caught the first train home—an earlier one than she'd said she'd catch, and so there was no one to meet her at the station. She rather liked doing that. Her aunt, she knew, was still paying visits to her relations, which made the homecoming even nicer.

"Glad to see you back, Miss," said the station-master, who was a great friend of hers.

"It's jolly nice to be back," sang Felicity cheerily. "They weren't expecting me till later, so there won't be anything to meet me."

"I'll ring up the 'All——" began the station-master.

"Oh, no," said Felicity. "I'll walk. Send up my box by the cart and I'll walk. I'm longing for a walk. Trains *are* such stuffy things, aren't they?"

The short cut from the station to the Hall lay across a field through a wood, across another field, over a stile and into a narrow lane.

As Felicity neared the stile she noticed a car coming down the lane. By the stile stood a man—a big man, cross-eyed and with great gorilla-like arms and hands. The lane was muddy. The car swept past the stile, sending a spurt of mud over the man. The occupant of the car turned a handsome face and laughed derisively at the appearance of his victim. A black trickle of mud dripped from the big man's nose. The car disappeared round the bend of the lane, its driver still laughing.

The man took out a grimy handkerchief and wiped his face.

"What a beast, Jakes!" said Felicity indignantly, lightly vaulting the stile into the lane.

The ferocious appearance imparted to the man by his cross-eyes and big arms was oddly at variance with the simple friendliness of his smile as he turned to Felicity.

"I reckon he didn't mean to do it, Miss Felicity," he said mildly, "it's main muddy, you know."

"Yes, but he needn't have *laughed*," said Felicity, still stern, "and he *might* have apologised."

"I guess I looked a bit funny, Miss," said Jakes mildly, still defending his absent assailant.

"Well, who is he, anyway?" said Felicity. "I've never seen him before. He doesn't live anywhere round here, does he?"

"I reckon he's the chap what's staying at The George," said Jakes slowly, "an actor chap, they do say."

"Well, I don't think much of him," said Felicity, closing her pretty lips very tight, "and it's all down your clothes."

"Eh, it'll brush off all right. Don't worry your head over it," smiled Jakes. "It's good to see you back, Miss. Have you enjoyed yourself away?"

Felicity's sternness disappeared and the dimples peeped out again.

"Yes," she said, "but it's *awfully* nice to get back."

She flitted up the wide shallow staircase of the Hall and listened for a moment outside her grandfather's door. It sounded rather a bad day. The door opened suddenly and Wakeman, his latest valet, came out. Crampton had left last week. There was a look of gloomy pleasure on Wakeman's face. Wakeman was a tall, thin, red-haired man with an unhealthy craving for excitement. He lived for Sir Digby's bad days and found his good ones very dull. He kept a little note-book, into which he entered all the names Sir Digby called him on his bad days (and Sir Digby only called him names on his bad days), and when he felt dull he read them over to himself. There was no cinema in Marleigh, but to Wakeman Sir Digby's bad days compensated for the lack.

Wakeman was just opening his note-book.

"Called me four quite new ones this morning, Miss," he said with gloomy pride.

"How lovely," said Felicity, "but if he's like that I don't think I'll go in, just yet."

She went downstairs to the library. Franklin looked up from his desk.

"Hello, Pins," he said. "You're a sight for sore eyes."

"Isn't it nice to be back?" she said, snatching oh her hat and throwing it on to a chair. "Tell me all the news . . . Aunt still away?"

"Yes."

"Well, let's thank Heaven for that," said Felicity piously. "And grandfather having a bad day . . . Oh, by the way, Frankie"—she seemed to remember something suddenly. "Do you know anything about anyone staying at The George—the sort of man who'd splash mud on people and then laugh at them? Nice-looking. An actor?"

"Oh—er—yes," said Franklin with a slight frown, "I know. A Mr. Boulton. He's been up here several times to see Mrs. Harborough."

"Mrs. Harborough? Is Violet staying here?"

"Yes. She arrived last week."

"And is this Mr. Boulton a friend of hers?"

"I gather so."

"All right, Frankie darling, if you want to be uncommunicative and unconfidential, be so. You're a materialist, as I'm always telling you. You haven't a soul above the morning's correspondence. Here am I, ready to discuss deep things of the spirit with you, and all you'll do is to eye the morning correspondence longingly and sadly, and say 'I gather so.' No, it's too late now. I'm going."

She went slowly to the morning-room to look for Violet. She was rather dismayed to hear that Violet was staying at the Hall. Violet had never come to the Hall before without John. Violet was essentially a "little woman." She screamed and fainted at the psychological moments and always clung to the nearest male for protection in times of danger. Felicity had not much use for her. Her chief virtue in Felicity's eyes was that she made John happy. Violet thought John the most wonderful man in all the world, and told him so in baby language at frequent intervals, gazing at him with adoring eyes and playing with his hair, or ears, or moustache as she did so. And, until lately, John had found time to repay all these compliments and endearments in kind, and life for the John Harboroughs had been one glad sweet song. Until lately. For Felicity had seen them not very long ago and had been conscious of a change. John was very busy and Violet had been peevish, bored and very sorry for herself. She felt neglected. Bereft of John's constant attention, she was scanning the horizon of her life for some fresh excitement. But—why on earth had she come to stay at Bridgeways without John? She'd never done that before. She'd always refused to go anywhere without John before.

The morning-room was empty. There was a broad cushioned seat in the window upon which Felicity loved to curl up. It was this morning sun-bathed and inviting. Felicity realised that she was sleepy. She'd gone to bed very late the night before and she'd got up very early that morning to see Priscilla off. So she curled up in the window-seat with the grace of a kitten and in a few minutes was fast asleep.

She awoke to hear two voices—one familiar, the other a stranger's.

"He neglects you. You can't deny it," said the strange voice. "I tell you you'll never regret it if you'll only come away with me. We'll go abroad. You do love me, don't you?"

"Oh, yes," said Violet's flute-like voice. "But——"

"But what?"

"He's coming this evening. He'll be here by seven. Perhaps—he'll be nicer to me then."

"No, he won't," said the other voice, "he lets you go away from him without a protest and expects you to be here meekly waiting for him when he chooses to come . . . Don't hesitate . . . I tell you, dearest, you'll never regret it. Meet me at the station here at half-past five . . . will you? We'll go away. I've arranged everything . . . We'll begin life afresh; will you? . . . will you? Promise."

"Yes," said Violet breathlessly.

Felicity realised suddenly that a screen completely hid her from the speakers and that she was eavesdropping. She put out a dainty foot and overbalanced the screen with a crash.

"Hello," she said, flushing slightly, her blue eyes moving from Violet to the man with her.

It was the man whom she had seen in the car in the lane, the man who had splashed Jakes with mud.

Violet gave a little scream.

"Felicity!" she said.

The man had gone rather pale.

"Ah," he said to Violet, "your sister-in-law?" Then to Felicity, "You've—er—interrupted a little rehearsal, Miss Harborough, that your sister-in-law and I are—I mean, we belong to an amateur dramatic society and we were rehearsing a little scene out of a play we are producing in the autumn."

He had recovered his poise quickly. His smile revealed a perfect set of teeth, and should have been a pleasant one, but somehow wasn't.

Felicity's clear-blue eyes met his squarely and his slid away.

"Shall we go on?" he said to Violet, "or have you had enough for this morning?"

"I've had enough," said Violet faintly.

"I'm sorry I disturbed you," said Felicity, leaping lightly to the ground, "I won't disturb you any longer."

She swung out of the room. They heard her whistling as she crossed the hall.

Felicity went into the garden. Despite of, or perhaps because of, her youth, her heart was large and loving and staunch and true. In spite of his pomposity she was fond of John, and because she was John's wife she was fond of Violet. She walked through the rose-garden, her brow drawn into a puzzled frown, her childish lips tight.

Then suddenly she stood still. Her brow cleared and her dimples peeped out. She clasped small brown firm hands and then broke into a little impromptu *pas seul*.

"I've got it, I've got it," she chanted joyously.

She walked slowly and demurely across the front lawn to where Mr. Boulton's manly form was outspread upon a deck-chair. Violet was not in sight.

Felicity dropped into an empty deck-chair beside him.

"Where's Violet?" she said.

"She's writing a letter," said the actor, "she'll be out soon."

"Are you tired after your rehearsal?" went on Felicity.

He shot her a suspicious glance, but Felicity's eyes were blue pools of innocence.

"Er—yes . . . I mean no . . . I mean slightly," said Mr. Boulton.

"How do you like Marleigh?" went on Felicity.

"Oh—so, so," said Mr. Boulton, looking at her with interest. Yes, she was a very pretty child. Very pretty indeed. "So, so."

"I suppose you don't know many of the people yet?"

"What people?"

"The village people. We've got some awfully interesting characters. Our blacksmith, Jakes, is the most interesting. He's—terrible!"

"Really?" said Mr. Boulton. "In what way terrible?"

"He's got the most *ferocious* temper. He's a great, enormous man with crossed eyes and long arms, and he's got such a ferocious temper that lots of people say he ought to be shut up. They say that no one with a temper like his can be quite sane."

Mr. Boulton's air of boredom dropped from him. He sat up and blinked.

"Eh?" he said.

"If he gets annoyed over anything," went on Felicity casually, "he won't rest till he's had his revenge, however long he has to wait. He's quite a mad man in that way. He's as strong as ten ordinary men, too. He's nearly killed several people round here who've annoyed him. People here would rather do anything on earth than annoy him."

Mr. Boulton was staring at her blankly.

94

"Eh?" he said again. "C-cross-eyed, did you say?"

"Yes," said Felicity innocently. "Cross-eyed and with dreadfully long arms. I saw him this morning in a fearful rage—almost out of his mind with rage—just because someone or other in a car had splashed mud over him and then laughed. He kept saying that he knew who it was and he'd be even with him before the day was out. I'm jolly sorry for whoever it was. He was smiling, and that's the worst sign of all with Jakes. When he smiles—it *looks* quite a gentle dreamy sort of smile— it means that he's in one of his most *ferocious* rages."

Mr. Boulton's mouth was still hanging open limply. He put up a finger as if to loosen his collar.

"D-did you say he *knew* the man who'd splashed him?" he said hoarsely.

"Oh, yes," said Felicity. Then she shuddered. "I'm so sorry for whoever it is . . . Well, here's Violet, so I'll go."

The look Mr. Boulton turned upon his (presumably) beloved was neither loving nor welcoming.

"C-cross-eyed," he murmured to himself, and added, "Good God!"

Felicity strolled across the lawn. Drewe, the gardener, approached her.

"I dunno what to put in those there two beds on the lawn, Miss Felicity," he said. "Sir Digby said he wanted somethin' diff'rent this year, but he didn't say what, an' Wakeman said he'd better not be asked about it to-day."

Imps of mischief danced in Felicity's blue eyes. Fate was certainly on her side.

"Let's have Jakes up and ask him," she said "He'll be able to help us."

Jakes, besides being the blacksmith, was the unofficial gardening expert of the village and Drewe's particular crony. Jakes' father had been gardener at the Hall and his advice was frequently sought by both Drewe and Sir Digby.

"Right, Miss," said Drewe, relieved, "then it sort of takes the responsibility off us like, don't it—case Sir Digby don't like it."

"That's the idea, Drewe," said Felicity. "Send one of the boys for him now."

Jakes, big and cross-eyed and ferocious-looking, arrived almost at once.

Felicity explained what was wanted. The imps of mischief in her blue eyes were like dancing stars. Fugitive dimples peeped in her cheeks as she spoke.

"I want you to go to the end of the lawn, Jakes," she said, "then you'll get the whole effect and you can see what will look best in those beds. Go just beyond those two deck-chairs where Mrs. Harborough and Mr. Boulton are and then you can judge."

"Right, Miss," said Jakes.

Jakes was very polite. He approached the two deckchairs humbly, a gentle smile on his lips, meaning to apologise to their occupants for his intrusion.

"You seem—different, somehow," Violet was saying to Mr. Boulton.

"How different?" said Mr. Boulton.

"You seem sort of *distrait*," said Violet. "I don't believe you love me at all. I believe you're beginning to be sorry you ever asked me to go away with you. You seem *restless*. You——"

Her companion looked up. His jaw dropped. His eyes dilated. An enormous cross-eyed man, wearing a gentle, dreamy smile, was approaching him over the lawn. Without a word he sprang from his chair, darted across the lawn and plunged headlong in at one of the open French windows of the library . . .

"So you think heliotropes, Jakes," said Felicity. "Thank you so much. I'll tell Drewe. And, Jakes, I want you to do something for me. You will, won't you?"

"Sure, Miss," said Jakes heartily.

"I'll tell you what it is."

She drew him behind the greenhouse and told him what it was. Jakes betrayed no surprise. Nothing ever surprised Jakes.

"Sure, Miss," was all he said.

If Felicity had asked him to walk round the garden on his hands, or plant bulbs with his teeth, he'd have said, "Sure, Miss," in just that tone of voice. And done it.

Felicity went across to Violet. "Do you think heliotropes would look nice in those beds, Violet?" she said.

"I'm sure I've no idea," said Violet tartly. "Wherever did Mr. Boulton go?"

"Underneath the table in the library," said Felicity innocently. "Shall I tell him you want him?"

But at that moment Mr. Boulton emerged, looking around first very cautiously, to make sure there was no sign of Jakes.

Felicity moved away as he approached. From the other end of the lawn, where she was engaged apparently in discussing the future contents of the garden-beds with Jakes, she watched them covertly. Violet looked sulky and Mr. Boulton, though evidently apologising profusely, seemed more anxious to keep a wary outlook round the garden than to placate his beloved.

Whistling softly, hands in her pockets, Felicity went up to them.

"I tell you it's nerves," Mr. Boulton was saying.

"They—they do take me like that sometimes. I can't help it."

"Well, all I can say is," replied Violet indignantly, "it's going to be very awkward for me—nerves taking you like that with no warning at all."

"They don't do it often——" he pleaded, and stopped as Felicity approached.

Felicity sank down gracefully at their feet.

"I say, Violet," she said earnestly, "*do* you think heliotropes would look all right in that bed? Jakes thinks they would."

"I don't know and I don't care," snapped Violet.

Felicity nibbled bits of grass in silence, lids lowered over downcast eyes. After a few seconds she leapt to her feet and walked away.

"Darling," said Mr. Boulton, as she departed, "this hasn't made any difference, has it? You—you'll meet me at the station at five-thirty, won't you?"

"Oh, yes," said Violet, but there was a disillusioned note in her voice, "though I must say I hope it doesn't take you like this often."

Mr. Boulton set out from The George at a quarter-to-five, gallantly determined to be at the station by five. He'd be glad to get away from Bridgeways. He'd had a most wearying day. He'd spent the first part of the afternoon appeasing Violet, and it had been most difficult. He'd had to begin all over again with the really hard spade-work—smiles, sighs, poetic language, protestation of undying affection, and all the rest of it. But it had been more or less successful.

Violet had agreed to overlook his momentary aberration and be at the station at half-past five, as though nothing had happened.

The second part of the afternoon he had spent barricaded in his hotel bedroom and watching the road, apprehensively, from behind his drawn blind. That terrible face—cross-eyes and gentle smile—was continually before his mind. That terrible sentence of Felicity's, "He's nearly killed several people round here who've annoyed him," was continually in his ears. Once, indeed, the terrible man had passed The George and Mr. Boulton had dived beneath his bed. But now—he'd only to walk to the station and all would be well. And it was only a few yards.

He walked slowly and warily. At a bend in the road he stopped and peeped cautiously about him. Good! The road was quite empty. The station was in sight. Then suddenly there appeared almost in front of him, and walking towards him, a large man with crossed eyes and long arms, wearing a gentle, dreamy smile. Jakes' instructions were to patrol the road between The George and the station from a quarter-to-five to five-thirty. He didn't know why and he didn't care why. Felicity had asked him to, and Felicity's word was law, and that was all there was to it.

At sight of him Mr. Boulton turned green and plunged into the nearest doorway.

It happened to be the Village Hall, where the vicar's daughter was conducting the Girls' Parish Club.

He met the blank gaze of a roomful of girls, and turned to dash out, ran into Jakes at the doorway and plunged back again.

Then he leant against the wall and looked around him, mopping his brow. Surely he wasn't awake. Surely it was all a nightmare. He pinched himself. He was awake. It wasn't a nightmare. It was all real. That awful man really was just outside waiting for him, waiting to kill him.

Suddenly Felicity stepped forward. Felicity was a member of the Girls' Club, though it must be admitted that she did not often attend the meetings. This afternoon, however, rather to everyone's surprise, she had appeared.

"Why, it's Mr. Boulton," said Felicity brightly. Then to the vicar's daughter, who was gazing open-mouthed at the vision of Mr. Boulton leaning against the wall and mopping his brow in the sacred precincts of the Girls' Parish Club, "Mr. Boulton's a famous London actor. I think he must have heard that we're without a speaker this afternoon, and come to tell us something about his work."

The vicar's daughter smiled and bridled.

"That will be delightful," she said, "will you speak from the platform, Mr. Boulton?"

A broken man, Mr. Boulton went up on to the platform.

Even the vicar's daughter, who was notoriously uncritical, said afterwards that it was incoherent. She said that from the very beginning she noticed something strange in the man's manner. Drugs, probably. Or drink. Often, in later life, the vicar's daughter would tell her more intimate friends of the occasion when she saw Frank Boulton, the actor, under the influence of drugs. Of course, she always added that it might have been drink, but she thought that it was drugs. As the vicarage was almost opposite the Green Man, she had had many opportunities of familiarising herself with the effects of drink upon the human male, and this was unlike anything she'd ever seen before. Quite unlike. Oh, most certainly, drugs.

After about ten minutes the address ended abruptly, and remarking that he had a train to catch, the lecturer descended from the platform before the vicar's daughter could collect her faculties to propose a vote of thanks. He opened the door, looked out, and plunging back again, leapt agilely upon the platform. He felt safer on higher ground.

"I've—er—just remembered some—er—other little details that—er—might interest you," he said, in a faint voice, his eyes fixed fearfully on the door. Then he plunged into a torrent of yet more incoherent speech. The climax of the drug effect, thought the vicar's daughter with interest. . . . Well, it was in a way an education to see what havoc drugs could wreak on a strong man's frame. But, on second thoughts, not very good for her flock.

"Thank you, Mr. Boulton," she said frigidly, when he paused for breath. "Thank you very much. We are now going to adjourn to the schools for tea. Er—thank you. Come, girls."

Keeping one eye fixed upon him (for it had just occurred to her that it might be neither drugs nor drink, but incipient insanity) she marshalled her flock out into the road and across to the schools.

Mr. Boulton was left alone. No, not quite alone. Felicity was there. Felicity had not accompanied the others to the schools. He edged behind the piano and, firmly barricaded there, spoke hoarsely to Felicity.

"Go and see if that man's still in the road," he said. "What man?" said Felicity innocently.

"The—the cross-eyed man," he said.

Felicity went to the door.

"Yes," she said, "he's still there."

"I must be at the station at five-thirty," moaned the actor, wringing his hands. "Oh, if only I'd got my makeup, I'd—I'd disguise myself, I'd——"

Felicity drew in her breath and again blue devils of mischief danced in her eyes. Fate really was on her side. She'd meant only to detain him till he was too late to keep his appointment. But now——After all, he'd suggested it himself.

"Oh, but there *is* make-up here," she said, "in the little room. It belongs to the Girls' Club Dramatic Society. I'm quite used to making people up. Here it is——"

"Quick," he panted, "there's only a few minutes. I can't be late. I tell you I can't be late."

She led him into a small inner room, opened a cupboard, and pulled out a box.

"Here's a beard," she said. "You fix it on while I make your face up."

"Do it quickly," he said desperately, "just disguise me . . . *any* way."

Felicity worked with frowning concentration. The actor himself could not see the effect. There was no mirror. He was too busy watching the door even to see what grease paints she used.

"Now you're quite disguised," she said.

"See if he's there."

She went out and joined the bored, but still amiable, Jakes in the road.

"Go and have a drink, Jakes," she said, "I'm sure you need it."

Jakes disappeared gratefully into The Green Man.

"No," said Felicity, re-entering the Village Hall, "he's not there."

Snatching up his bag, Mr. Boulton ran with all his might down the road towards the station.

Violet was annoyed. She'd waited quite five minutes for him, and she wasn't used to waiting quite five minutes for anyone. Certainly John had never kept her waiting for quite five minutes . . .

Suddenly she saw someone running down the road. It wasn't . . . Oh, it couldn't be. . . . Her face grew pale with horror . . . it was a man—a straggly, grey beard floated in the wind. His cheeks were whitened, his nose was vermilioned. His front hair was greased into three little spikes that stuck up in a row. Strange hieroglyphics in brown grease paints adorned his brow. . . . Felicity had done her work well . . .

He arrived panting.

"Here I am, darling," he said, "I hope I'm not very late."

She started back with a scream, dropping umbrella and bag in the road

"Oh, you *brute*," she cried. "How *dare* you!"

Then without another word she turned and ran back to the Hall.

Mr. Boulton, bewildered and breathless, picked up her umbrella and bag and looked down the road.

Jakes was just emerging from The Green Man. With a moan Mr. Boulton slipped through a hedge into a field and hid behind a tree.

He arrived at the Hall a quarter-of-an-hour later.

He carried a lady's umbrella in one hand and a lady's bag in the other, and a host of explanations in his brain. His beard had come oil in the hedge, but the rest of the make-up retained its first fine, careless rapture.

The last hour had been so crowded with inglorious life that the actor himself had forgotten the trifling incident of his disguise. He fondly imagined himself the matinee idol who generally met his eyes when he looked into his mirror.

The big front door was open. He walked into the hall.

It happened that Sir Digby was just coming downstairs.

He was feeling slightly better, but only slightly.

At sight of the strange intruder he stood petrified with astonishment half-way down the stairs.

Mr. Boulton advanced with his famous charming smile. "Excuse me," he began.

Sir Digby's face went purple, his eyes bulged, then he burst out in a ferocious rage.

"Get out, sir," he bellowed. "How *dare* you come Christie Minstrelling in a gentleman's house? Do you take this for a music-hall? I tell you, you're drunk, sir. GET OUT!"

Mr. Boulton's spirit was broken by the events of the afternoon and Sir Digby's outburst of rage was the last straw.

He turned with a low moan and fled back to the station a train was just on the point of starting for London, and this seemed to Mr. Boulton to be a direct intervention of Providence on his behalf. He leapt into it thankfully just as the train was moving out of the station he realised that he still carried Violet's bag and umbrella. He flung them viciously out on to the platform.

Felicity leant out of her bedroom window. Beneath her, on the lawn, were two shadowy figures, which she recognised as those of her brother John and her sister-in-law Violet. John had arrived just before dinner and had been greeted by his wife with an affection that surprised him. Felicity could see, in the dusk, that Violet's head was on John's shoulder and that John's arms were round her. Their voices, hushed and indistinguishable, rose in whispers through the evening air . . .

"And then he went mad, darling," Violet was saying.

"Mad?"

"Yes—ever so mad . . . Oh, John, he arrived at the station to elope with me in a sort of carnival get-up—a funny beard and a funny hat, and a red nose. . . . quite mad, and then I realised, darling, that I could never really love anyone but you, you . . . You *do* forgive me, don't you?"

"Darling," said the loyal John, "I blame myself entirely . . ." Then, after a pause:

"Nobody—er—knew, darling, did they?"

"Oh no, John."

"Not Felicity?"

"Oh *no*, John . . . she's such a child . . . Why, John, you'd hardly believe it, but with this terrible drama going on before her eyes Felicity didn't give a thought to *anything*, not to *anything*, but those wretched flower-beds on the lawn."

Chapter Seven

Felicity Comes to Town

"Marcia wants me to go and stay with her in town,' said Felicity, waving a letter in the air.

"We must bear in mind, Felicity," said Lady Montague firmly, "that you are yet in the schoolroom."

Felicity stopped waving the letter.

"I'm sixteen," she said with dignity.

"The fact remains," said Felicity's aunt crushingly, "that you have not yet come out."

"I know," said Felicity, swinging herself up lightly upon the table, "but nowadays it doesn't matter. I mean nowadays you don't come out with a bang like you used to. You unfold gradually like a flower. It's much more poetical. I read somewhere the other day that nowadays girls begin to go out to dinner when they're fifteen, and when they're sixteen they begin to go to dances and night clubs and drink cocktails, and when they're seventeen they do all those things till they're simply sick of them, and when they're eighteen someone gives a dance to mark the fact that life has no further experiences to offer them."

"Felicity," said Lady Montague, "I can hardly believe my ears. You should not know the meaning of such a word as cocktail!"

"Oh, but don't you think I should, aunt?" said Felicity earnestly. "I mean, how can I spurn it with lofty scorn when someone offers it to me if I don't know the difference between it and lemonade. I know a cocktail quite well. It has a little stick in it with a cherry on the end."

"I am glad to say," said Lady Montague, with dignity, "that—er—the beverage we are discussing has never passed my lips."

Felicity tossed her red-gold head.

"It hasn't mine either, aunt," she said, and added hopefully—"yet."

Marcia was Felicity's married sister. Every August Felicity went away to the seaside with Marcia and her family because August was the Parliamentary vacation, and Matthew, Marcia's husband, who was a Cabinet Minister, and a very important personage, sent his secretary away for his holiday then, and played at being a private individual. This year, however, he had to stay in town to attend some important meetings, so his family arranged to stay with him. Marcia thought it would be a nice change for Felicity to stay with them in town. So did Felicity. Lady Montague, however, was not quite so sure. She disapproved of any excitement for Felicity, and she disapproved of London.

"I'll speak to your grandfather about the invitation, Felicity," she said, "and we will abide by his decision."

She found Sir Digby Harborough in a very bad mood indeed. Lady Montague always bowed before Sir Digby's storms like a willow in the wind.

"If the child wants to go, let her go," roared Sir Digby, "let her go—let *her* go!"

"Certainly," said Lady Montague hastily. "I was not purposing to put any obstacle in the way. Only she is young and headstrong and——"

"Let her go!" roared Sir Digby, suddenly turning purple in the face.

"Exactly what I was suggesting," said Lady Montague, retiring as precipitately as was compatible with her dignity.

The muffled sounds of Sir Digby's growling pursued her down the corridors.

Sir Digby could and did growl threateningly for hours on end on his bad days.

Felicity ran into the drawing-room. Rosemary was there writing a letter at the writing-table. Rosemary was on one of her rare visits to her grandfather's home. She looked, as usual, beautiful and haughty with something of bitterness and weariness behind the hauteur and oddly at variance with her youth. But her glance softened as it rested on Felicity.

"Rosemary darling," said Felicity, "isn't it fun! I'm going to London to stay with Marcia."

"Goodness! Is Aunt Marcella letting you? I thought she didn't approve of London for the young."

"She doesn't, but grandfather was in a good temper and said I might. Won't it be *fun?*"

"When are you going?"

"Next week."

"I shall be putting in a few days with Marcia then," said Rosemary, frowning meditatively. "So we may meet there."

"If we do, darling," said Felicity, pleading, "you won't boss me, will you? Promise."

Rosemary smiled. She didn't smile very often, but she had a very beautiful smile.

"I promise," she said.

Felicity went into the library where Franklin sat writing.

"I'm going to London! I'm going to London! I'm going to London!" she chanted. "I'm going to London to lead the fast life. I'm going to drink cocktails and go to night clubs and smoke cigarettes. Won't it be fun!"

"Don't, Pins; you're making me dizzy! Stay still a second. When are you going and where are you going and why are you going?"

"I'm going next week and I'm going to London to Marcia's. Rosemary's going to be there part of the time."

"Oh, well," said Franklin, trying not very successfully to speak casually, as he always did when Rosemary was mentioned. "I suppose she'll keep you in order."

"No, she won't!" said Felicity triumphantly. "She's promised not to."

Felicity arrived at Marcia's and Matthew's house in Westminster at the end of the week.

Marcia was nice. So were Marcia's children, Micky and Primula.

Marcia's husband, Matthew, too, was nice, in spite of his being a very important personage.

Felicity spent the first evening in the nursery playing with Micky and Primula. Primula had an electric train with stations, and Felicity, despite her sixteen years, enjoyed playing with trains. She sat cross-legged on the carpet, and made the train's more exciting noises, and had brilliant ideas about fashioning stations out of cardboard boxes and little extra passengers out of rags and matches. She even made little tickets, which Primula and Micky had never thought of, and a little thing to punch them with made out of a pin. Micky and Primula loved her dearly. They called her "Auntifisty" all in one word.

"Perhaps you'd rather they didn't call you aunt," said Marcia. "It's more fashionable not to, I believe." Felicity threw back her glorious plait and raised her blue eyes from the miniature train tickets.

"Oh *no*," she said, "*do* let them call me 'aunt.' I love it. It makes me feel so *old*."

Matthew (who was tall and thin and slightly bald and always wore eyeglasses and a buttonhole) took his duties as Felicity's host very seriously.

"Is there anything you'd like to do to-day, Pins?" he said to her, somewhat apprehensively, at lunch.

"Yes," said Felicity firmly, "I'd like to go out somewhere. Somewhere fast. I've never been fast, and I want to try being it."

He gave a resigned sigh. "A night club, I suppose?" he said. "Very well, I'll do my best."

He did his best. He arranged to take her to a night club directly after dinner. The whole onus of the undertaking was to fall upon him, because Marcia had another engagement so could not go with them. Felicity kept him waiting for some time, and when she appeared she took away his breath. Over her plain white georgette dress she wore a gorgeous silver tissue cloak of Marcia's. Her red-gold hair was taken up and massed in plaits at the back of her shapely little head.

"By Jove!" he said, beneath his breath, because he hadn't realised before quite how lovely Felicity was.

Marcia laughed.

"What *would* Aunt Marcella say?" she said.

"She wouldn't say anything," said Felicity, "she'd just curl up and die."

It was a very gorgeous room. People were dancing in the middle of it and round the sides people sat at little tables.

"What shall we do first?" said Matthew.

A cocktail first," said Felicity very firmly.

He ordered a cocktail. People were looking at Felicity with interest. Although she wasn't a stunning beauty like Rosemary, still you wouldn't see anything much prettier than Felicity in a week's journey. Felicity soon disposed of the male starers. At the glance they received from her blue eyes, they looked hastily and sheepishly away again. Felicity had plenty of spirit and disliked being stared at.

"Well?" said Matthew, when she had finished the cocktail.

"I didn't like the taste much," said Felicity critically," and I think it's given me a headache. I'll try a cigarette now."

In silence he handed her his cigarette case. Felicity took one and looked at it closely.

"Does it matter much which end you light?" she said.

"It's usual to have the cork end in your mouth," said Matthew.

He lit it for her.

"Do they all taste like this?" said Felicity. She spoke in a disillusioned tone of voice.

"More or less," said Matthew.

"I'd thought it was different, somehow," sighed Felicity.

"Well, we're getting on with it, aren't we?" she said, as she finished it, in the tone of one whose dogged determination is carrying her through a herculean task.

"With what?" said her brother-in-law.

"With the fast life," said Felicity. "Shall we dance now?"

*

When Marcia entered the nursery the next morning she found Felicity sitting on the floor with Micky and Primula. They had made a drink consisting of the juices of an orange and a lemon, with the addition of some sherbet and plenty of sugar and were drinking it with relish.

"It's lovely," said Felicity, "it's heaps nicer than the cocktail."

"How did you enjoy last night, darling?" said Marcia, who had been out when they came home and had breakfasted in bed.

"I didn't," said Felicity with great conviction. "Cocktails are just like medicine, and cigarettes are like a Channel crossing. I like myself much better this morning. We're frightfully busy getting ready a hospital because there's been a most horrible accident on the line, and hundreds and thousands of the passengers are wounded."

"Here's a stretcher, Auntifisty," said Primula, solemnly.

"Oh, by the way, Rosemary's coming to-day," said Marcia.

"Is she?" said Felicity, looking up with interest from her cardboard hospital. "What fun. Or rather, I don't suppose we shall see much of her, shall we? We never do."

"Someone else is coming, too," said Marcia, "a Mr. Markson."

"Who's he?" said Felicity, skilfully fashioning a bed out of a matchbox and some matches.

"Well, an old school friend of Matthew's wrote and asked Matthew to invite him. He's an American, and he's writing a book on English Parliamentary institutions, or something of the sort. It's to be a sort of standard reference book, and I suppose he thought that Matthew might help him."

"I don't suppose he'll do much writing of standard reference books while Rosemary's about," said Felicity wisely. "People don't, you know."

"One of dem's killed dead, Auntifisty," said Micky solemnly. "The twain went over his tummy."

"Oh, we'll have a funeral, then," said Felicity in her most businesslike fashion.

Rosemary arrived just before Mr. Markson.

She greeted Felicity casually. "How's the family?" she said.

"Splendid!" said Felicity cheerfully. "Aunt Marcella's got a cold and so hasn't been up to see us since Sunday. It's an ill wind. . . . Grandfather's got an awfully bad attack this morning. Even in the distance he sounds like a pack of lions. And Frankie says——"

Rosemary raised her eyebrows. "Frankie?"

"Mr. Franklin," said Felicity impatiently. "This morning he——"

"I'm afraid I'm not interested in Mr. Franklin," said Rosemary. And just then Mr. Markson came.

Mr. Markson was middle-aged and handsome in a florid style, with a very slight foreign accent, which he said was the result of long sojourn in foreign countries. No one seemed to like him very much. He was pathetically grateful to Matthew for offering him hospitality. He said that he'd tried to work in hotels and rooms and boarding-houses and couldn't. He wanted, he said, to make his book an eternal monument to the excellence of English Parliamentary Institutions.

Like most men he seemed restless when Rosemary was anywhere in his neighbourhood. In spite of her completely ignoring him he constantly and languishingly fixed his large flashing dark eyes upon her.

The first evening of his visit Matthew took them all to the theatre. Aunt Marcella's ideas of How a Young Girl should be Brought Up did not include visits to the theatre, and so Felicity had seen very few plays. This one turned out to be a play that Rosemary dismissed contemptuously as "tripe," Marcia as "slush," and Mr. Markson as "perhaps a little tee-dious." Matthew slept peacefully from the beginning of the first scene to the end of the last, so his opinion does not count. Felicity, however, was thrilled by it. Its heroine was very beautiful, and very proud and very haughty. She was in love with the hero, but in the power of the villain, because of some indiscreet letters she had once written to him. So the heroine's young sister determined to secure the letters for her and visited the villain's bedroom to get them. Of course the villain came in while she was searching for them, but she slipped behind the window curtain. Then the villain foolishly

110

stepped into a large cupboard in the wall where he kept his clothes and the young sister boldly and bravely slammed the door of it and turned the key. Then a lot of things happened. Other people came in and someone shot someone and it was all very confusing and exciting, but in the end the proud heroine was left in the arms of the handsome hero while the young sister smiled serenely and beneficently upon the reward of her bravery.

Felicity was so thrilled that she could scarcely attend to anything anyone said at the supper afterwards. At first she saw herself as the haughty heroine and emulated her in speech and manner to her own complete satisfaction till Marcia said:

"What's the matter, dear?"

Felicity blushed. "Nothing. Why?"

"I thought perhaps you'd got toothache or a headache or something," said Marcia solicitously.

"Oh, no," said Felicity, slightly annoyed. "I'm quite all right."

This discouraged her as far as the heroine was concerned. But the role of the young sister was left.

For the next few days, as she played with Micky and Primula in the nursery, or went about with Marcia and Rosemary and Matthew, she lived through all the thrilling scenes in imagination. She entered the bedrooms of villains a dozen times a day in search of letters written to them by Rosemary. For Rosemary, beautiful and cold and remote, was in every way a most satisfactory heroine.

Then quite suddenly the situation she had dealt with so often and so satisfactorily in imagination occurred.

She was passing the drawing-room door one day, on her way to the nursery, when she heard Rosemary's voice, saying:

"Please give them back to me."

And Mr. Markson:

"Certainly not."

Felicity's heart leapt. Mr. Markson, of course, had some compromising letters of Rosemary's and was refusing to return them. It was the only explanation of the words. The scene was laid. It only remained for her to creep into Mr. Markson's room and extract the letters from—from wherever he kept them (that

111

part might be rather difficult, of course) . . . and lock him up in his cupboard if he interrupted her in the middle. There was a large cupboard made into the wall in his room. Felicity's spirits rose at the thought. Everything seemed to fit in beautifully. But, of course, she must choose a moment when he was not in the house, and that at first seemed an almost insuperable difficulty. For Mr. Markson seemed never to be out of the house. He spent all the day alone in the library writing his book and in the evening discussed with Matthew the Parliamentary Institutions of Great Britain. Matthew had said that if he stayed much longer he, Matthew, would be driven to blow up the Houses of Parliament or do something really drastic to upset the Parliamentary Institutions of Great Britain, because they were getting on his nerves. It was rather a relief to everyone when Mr. Markson announced that day at lunch that he must go home on Saturday.

Felicity decided that there was no time to be lost. She must get the letters at once, even at the risk of his interrupting her. She could always lock him into his cupboard, of course . . .

She crept upstairs to the bedroom landing. No one was there. Rosemary was out. Marcia was lying down; the children were in the nursery. She opened Mr. Markson's bedroom door and slipped into the room with beating heart. She looked round fearfully. Where on earth did one begin looking for letters? She'd no idea, but she must do something quickly. He might come in any minute. She opened a few drawers—collars and shirts and handkerchiefs and things. She began seriously to doubt the wisdom of having come in at all. But still—now that she'd come she wasn't going away till she'd got them. She opened his trunk. It was empty. She opened a small wooden box. It was empty. She was just going to close it when a sound outside startled her and she stumbled, falling forward into the box with her hands outspread. Her heart began to race violently as she stood up, her eyes fixed on the door. But the sound had died away. It had only been a maid coming to shut the landing window. Felicity looked down at the box and her eyes opened wide with surprise. In her fall she had touched some spring and half of the bottom of the box was rolling away, revealing a small secret recess in the false bottom.

And there were the letters.

Felicity grabbed them and went quickly out of the room, closing the door very silently behind her. The landing was empty. Clutching the papers tightly she flitted down the great wide staircase. And there at the bottom was Rosemary, just coming in at the front door, looking very beautiful in her dark hat and furs. Felicity handed her the bundle of papers.

"There!" she said dramatically.

In the play the heroine had flung herself into the young sister's arms with sobs of gratitude. But Rosemary didn't. She stared at Felicity and then said:

"What on earth is it?"

"The letters," said Felicity.

"What letters?" said Rosemary.

Real life was very disappointing.

"The letters you want," said Felicity impatiently.

"But I don't want any letters," said Rosemary. "I get far more than I can possibly answer as it is."

"But—but you said—I heard you saying to Mr. Markson—you said, 'Please give them back to me,' and he said 'Certainly not!'"

Rosemary considered.

"Oh, yes," she said at last, "I remember. Marcia had given him some silly snaps of the children, and I was in some of them and I didn't want him to have those because he seemed to be getting rather foolish, that's all."

Felicity went slowly into the drawing-room. She'd made a mistake. Things never turn out the way you mean them to. She'd taken a lot of trouble and this was all the reward she got for it. No one wanted the letters now she'd got them. Rosemary was a most unsatisfactory heroine. And now she'd have to take them back. She'd tried living a fast life and she'd tried taking the star part in a melodrama and both had fallen flat. She'd rather play at trains with Micky and Primula any day, thought Felicity, with a disillusioned shake of her red-gold head. No one wanted the letters now she'd got them.

She wandered mournfully into the empty drawing-room to think out the situation. Yes, the only thing to do was to put them back where she'd found them.

The door opened and with a guilty start Felicity slipped the little pile of papers on to Marcia's writing-table. She felt that anything was better than being caught by anybody with the papers in her hand.

But it was only Rosemary.

"Where's Marcia?" she said.

"I think she's lying down," said Felicity.

She waited till all was quiet again and then slipped upstairs to the fatal bedroom. There was far less elation in the proceeding this time. She'd be jolly glad when the whole thing was over. She was simply sick of Mr. Markson and Rosemary and their letters, and wished she hadn't tried to help them. She'd never try to get anyone's incriminating letters back for them again, never in all her life. The bedroom was still empty, thank heaven. She went over to the box by the window and slipped her hand into her pocket for the papers. Her pocket was empty. She'd left them on Marcia's writing-table, where she'd put them when Rosemary came into the room. Not the slightest doubt that Felicity, who was generally equal to any situation, was getting "rattled." And then just when she was wondering what on earth to do came the click of the bedroom door. It opened slowly. Someone was coming into the room.' Felicity hastily withdrew into the shelter of the heavy window curtains. It was Mr. Markson. She could see his funny foreign-looking face and black shiny head. He did not see her. He went across to the cupboard in the wall. He opened the door and stepped in to get something that hung on a hook. A coat, probably. It was all exactly as it had happened in the play. It was too much for Felicity. The force of association was too strong. Like a flash she darted forward, slammed the door and turned the key in the lock. He didn't shout or bang on the door as she expected he would, but she could hear him fiddling about with the lock inside, trying to open it.

And she went swiftly downstairs for the papers. She realised that she was making a distinct mess of the affair. Look at it in any way she would, she had to admit that she was making a distinct mess of it. She had taken the papers without making sure that they were Rosemary's and—and they'd turned out not to be. They might have been, of course, but the fact remained that they weren't. Then she'd gone upstairs to put the letters back and left them behind on Marcia's writing-table. Then she'd locked him in the cupboard. She didn't know how she was going to explain that to him. In fact, she didn't know how she was going to explain anything to him. In fact, she didn't know how she was going to explain anything to anyone, and she saw the moment when explanations would be demanded not far ahead.

She entered the drawing-room. Matthew stood by the table reading the papers. Her luck was absolutely out, thought Felicity with a resigned sigh. She'd have to make a clean breast of it now.

Matthew was looking rather queer.

"Do you know anything about these papers, Pins?" he said.

"They—they belong to Mr. Markson," said Felicity calmly. Then came a wild hope that she needn't return them . . . perhaps they were only washing bills and perhaps she could just send in a maid or the gardener to unlock his cupboard and explain that it had been done by accident. "Are they important?" she said.

Matthew crossed the room and closed the door.

"They are rather," he said drily, "they're copies of very important political papers that must have been taken from the safe in the library by someone who knows the combination. Markson, you say? . . . He must—Good Lord! of course . . . he's no more writing a book on—and he's been in there every blessed day . . . Who got these from him?"

"I did, Matthew," said Felicity.

"And where is the blackguard?" said Matthew. "Bolted?"

Felicity conquered an inclination to giggle.

"No, Matthew. He—he's quite safe. I've locked him in his wardrobe."

*

Felicity had returned home from her visit. She walked into the library still wearing her outdoor things. Franklin looked up from his writing-table and smiled a welcome.

"Hello," said Felicity, "I've come back. Don't say 'So I see.'"

"All right. I won't," he said, clearing a place for her on the writing-table. He knew that Felicity preferred tables to chairs. "I'll say instead that I'm very glad to see you. And mean it. Your aunt is out. Your grandfather is in bed—so you'll have to share my humble tea in here. It's due any minute. What sort of a time have you had?"

"Great!" said Felicity. "I've drunk deep of all life's experiences, Frankie. I've lived a fast life and found that it's all dust and ashes. I mean, it tastes like medicine and makes you feel sick."

"Really?" said Franklin with a twinkle.

Moult entered with the tea.

"Hello, Moult, darling," said Felicity. "I've come back."

Moult threw her a pained glance. He disapproved equally of her mode of address and her position upon the desk.

"So I see, Miss," he said.

Felicity heaved a deep satisfied sigh.

"I knew you'd say that, Moult," she said. "I'd have felt frightfully disappointed if you hadn't done."

"Pour out, there's a good girl," said Franklin, as the door closed behind Moult.

"I'm horribly hungry," said Felicity pathetically as she poured out.

"A curious story about you has reached me, Pins," he said, as he took his cup.

"What was it?" said Felicity, nibbling toast.

"The story went that, single-handed, you attacked an anarchist or spy or something of that sort, forced him to surrender his incriminating documents, locked him in a cupboard, and then went off to fetch Scotland Yard to him."

Felicity gurgled.

"It sounds awfully nice put that way, Frankie, but if you'll let me eat your share of the toast, as well as mine, I'll tell you in confidence what really happened."

She had both shares of the toast.

He enjoyed the story of what really happened just as much as she'd meant him to. But at the end he became grave. He was obviously going to ask her something, then obviously checked himself.

And Felicity knew that he wanted to ask her about Rosemary.

But because Felicity was beginning to understand about Franklin and Rosemary, and because she was very, very sorry for him about it (because men always fell in love with Rosemary and Rosemary was hateful to them all), she did not mention Rosemary and soon slipped away; leaving him to his work.

Chapter Eight

Felicity and the Poet

"Felicity, dear," said Lady Montague. She looked up with a pleased smile from a letter she was reading. A pleased smile was as rare a visitant to her ladyship's countenance as is an altruism to a crocodile's heart.

"Felicity, dear," she repeated, "an old school friend of mine is taking The Grange for a month. It will be delightful to have her so near, though I haven't seen her for years and years. She married one of the Elthams of Hampshire."

Her niece groaned. Lady Montague's Somebodies of Somewhere were always so dull . . .

"And she has a son," went on her ladyship.

Felicity groaned again.

"Such a *brilliant* boy," added Lady Montague.

"I suppose it's his mother who tells you that," said Felicity.

"Yes," said Lady Montague, and then added rather indignantly as if sensing some criticism in Felicity's tone, "After all, Felicity, it's a mother who knows her son best. They'll be in residence to-day," she went on, as if they were the Royal Family. "I must go and call on them at once. You'd better come with me, Felicity."

"It's my elocution lesson this afternoon," said Felicity hastily. "I—I think I'd better go to it now."

She escaped hastily before her aunt could say anything else.

Mrs. Graves, the elocution mistress, was waiting for her.

Mrs. Graves was very dignified and very, very large. But in spite of this, or perhaps because of this, she elocuted magnificently. She could and did move her diaphragm in and out like a concertina with no apparent effort at all. She made most casual remarks about the weather or the train service in a voice that would have wrung the hearts of an audience if used by Lady Macbeth in the sleep-walking scene. It was Lady Montague who had engaged her. Lady Montague considered that every lady should be able to produce her voice correctly. So far the lessons had (fortunately) made no appreciable difference in Felicity's own voice, but Felicity could give an excellent imitation of her instructress and could remark that it was a fine day in a voice so fraught with tragedy and pathos that it was difficult to listen to it unmoved.

"Gooder morninger, Feeleecity," said Mrs. Graves, exploding her consonants, distending her diaphragm, and speaking in a voice of heart-rending emotion.

"Gooder morninger, Mrs. Graves," said Felicity demurely in the same tone of voice.

Mrs. Graves threw her pupil a quick glance. She sometimes suspected that Felicity's imitation was not the sincerest form of flattery.

"Now, Feeleecity," said Mrs. Graves, "you see this instrument on the table. Eet is called a phonograph. Eet records the human voice." Mrs. Graves said this in the tone in which Hamlet might have addressed his mother. "By eet you may see your rate of progress." In this tone might Romeo have taken a long farewell of Juliet. "I will leave the instrument here and I propose that this week"—for a moment Mrs. Graves' voice seemed to die away with emotion, then she mastered herself—"that for this week, Feeleecity, you say a veerse of poetry into eet every day—I will show you how eet works before I go—and when I come again we will play the records," thus might Julius Caesar dying have addressed Brutus, "and see how you improve day by day. Let us begin at once, Feeleecity. Will you now recite into the instrument any great poem of our wonderful, wonderful English language."

Felicity thought for a moment and then recited clearly:

"Old Noah he had an ostrich farm and fowls on the largest scale,

He ate his egg with a ladle in an egg-cup big as a pail.

And the soup he took was Elephant Soup and the fish he took was Whale.

But they all were small to the cellar he took when he set out to sail.

And Noah he often said to his wife when he sat down to dine:
'I don't care where the water goes if it doesn't get into the wine.'"

"That will do, Feeleecity," said Mrs. Graves coldly, "I don't know why you should quote a poem by a man with whose views on the Temperance question I entirely disagree when you might have quoted any of the beautiful poems I have taught you."

"Because I like it," said Felicity simply.

The elocution lesson ended. There was just time for a walk before tea, so Felicity went for a walk.

And on the common she met Sheila. Sheila hasn't been mentioned before simply because she doesn't happen to have come into the story before, but she was the daughter of a novelist who lived in the next village, and she was just a little older than Felicity, and Felicity was very fond of her. Sheila had dark hair and dark velvety eyes, smooth rosy cheeks and a dimple. Felicity hailed her with a whoop of joy. As I have said, Felicity liked Sheila. And Felicity suspected that Ronald liked Sheila even more than she did, and Sheila, in Felicity's eyes, was the only girl she had ever met whom she considered worthy of Ronald, so Felicity felt happy.

They walked together along the common. Sheila was, as ever, lighthearted and radiant, but to-day Felicity thought her light-heartedness and radiance slightly—very slightly—dimmed.

"Is anything the matter, Sheila?" said Felicity.

"Of course not . . . Ronald's not at home, is he?"

"No."

The clock in the village church chimed "four" and Felicity, who had quite a range of vulgar exclamations, said: "Oh, *Crikey*!" and hastened home.

Lady Montague was radiant.

"I paid my call at The Grange this afternoon,' she said to Felicity.

"It was a most delightful visit. *So* nice to see dear Mrs. Eltham again. And her dear son was there."

Felicity displayed no curiosity about her dear son, so Lady Montague continued:

"He's a *brilliant* boy," she went on, "a poet. There, Felicity, you'll be able, to see a real live poet!"

"What's he written?" said Felicity, unimpressed.

"Poems, of course," said Lady Montague rather impatiently, and added: "And they're coming to tea to-morrow afternoon, Felicity. Perhaps you'd recite one of those beautiful poems Mrs. Graves teaches you, dear. Being a poet, he might like it. Something—poetical, you, know. I've never heard you recite yet, and after all those lessons you ought to be able to . . . Something beautiful, you know, and, of course, refined. Something out of dear Tennyson, such as 'We are Seven,' or—or 'The Boy Stood on the Burning Deck,' or—what was it?—'The Wreck of the Little Revenge.'"

Marmaduke Percival Eltham was an only son. He had been guarded and treasured and shielded from life's rough winds from his earliest infancy. He had not been sent to a public school because it was felt that life's rough winds might blow upon him in a public school. He had been educated by tutors who "understood" him. His mother had had great difficulty in finding tutors who "understood" him. "Understanding" Marmaduke Percival meant accepting his monkey tricks as "high spirits," his stupidity as "genius," his cheek as "wit," and perpetually conquering your inclination to smack his head. His mother was a woman of determination and she dismissed tutor after tutor till she found one who, on consideration of a soft job and a large salary, was willing to "understand" Marmaduke.

Marmaduke had decided to be a poet when he was six years old and he had watched a celebrated poet who was staying in the house. The poet didn't seem to do anything but talk, and everyone crowded round him hanging upon his words. It seemed to Marmaduke to be a pleasant calling. When he was twelve his mother gave him a rhyming dictionary, but he found it less trouble to do it without rhymes, and when he was nineteen he actually

121

had a poem printed in a paper. It was mother-love that wrought the miracle. Mrs. Eltham gave a large subscription to the funds of the paper on condition that the editor accepted Marmaduke's poem and put it on the front page. She could not get him to repeat the experiment, however, because he said that he lost far more from the subsequent falling-off of his subscribers than she had given him . . .

So Marmaduke had all his little poems printed in a little book bound in white vellum and with his name in gold on the outside. He didn't submit them to editors or publishers because editors and publishers are nasty, unkind, unsympathetic men and didn't "understand" him. Instead, he had them printed at his mother's expense, which was far less trouble for everyone concerned.

You are not prepared, after all this, to hear that Marmaduke was nice-looking, but he was. He was quite handsome in a Byronic style, and he always wore a flowing tie and his dark curly hair just a little longer than other people wore it, to heighten the effect.

They arrived quite early in the afternoon. His mother introduced him with pride, and Lady Montague said: "*There,* Felicity! Now you can say that you've met a real poet," and Marmaduke simpered and Felicity looked sphinx-like. Then Lady Montague talked to Mrs. Eltham and Marmaduke sat back and looked like a poet, occasionally arranging his hair and his tie and casting furtive glances of admiration at Felicity's delicate porcelain face with its speedwell-blue eyes, its rosebud mouth, and its frame of red-gold hair. And Felicity sat and looked dreamily before her . . .

Then Sheila came in. It was Felicity who noticed Sheila's sudden confusion when she saw the poet.

"Oh, we've met before," said Marmaduke, with an oily smile.

Sheila, her pretty face flushed, tried to carry off the situation with a conventional greeting but only partially succeeded.

Felicity looked from one to the other, frowning pensively, her tawny plait over her shoulder.

"A real *poet,* my dear," said Lady Montague proudly to Sheila.

Felicity noticed that Sheila avoided the poet's eyes and that her lips tightened whenever she heard his voice. His voice certainly was not a pleasant one. It was shrill and piercing. It was in every way disappointing. It did not go at all with his Byronic appearance.

Sheila made an excuse to depart soon after tea and Felicity ran out after her and overtook her in the drive.

"Sheila, darling," said Felicity, slipping her arm through Sheila's, "what's the matter? Do tell me."

She led her as she spoke by a narrow path away from the drive and towards the greenhouses.

"I must go home, Felicity," said Sheila, making an ineffectual effort to return to the drive.

"No, you mustn't," said Felicity firmly, "not before you've told me what the matter is, anyway."

Sheila smiled down at her—a rather unsteady smile.

"I can't, Felicity darling . . . You're—such a baby."

Felicity drew her slim young body up to its full height.

"I'm sixteen," she said with dignity.

"What's he doing here?" said Sheila, "that man, I mean."

"Marmaduke Percival?" said Felicity. "They've taken The Grange. Aunt's awfully bucked because she was at school with the Mamma. They're going to poison the atmosphere for about a month, I believe . . . Where did you know him before, Sheila?"

She opened a greenhouse door. "It's beautifully fuggy in here," she said, "and we can sit on flower pots and watch the grapes grow and you can tell me all about it."

Sheila smiled, though quite obviously she didn't feel like smiling. She looked at Felicity, who was already sitting upon a large upturned flower pot. Her eyes wandered slowly down Felicity's figure in its workmanlike Fair Isle jumper and short tweed skirt.

"You *are* nice, Felicity," she said at last.

"If I'm nice, tell me, then," pleaded Felicity.

Sheila sat down upon the flower pot next Felicity's.

"I will, Felicity," she said with sudden resolve. "You'll think me a blamed fool, but I just can't help that. I am. I mean, I was. It was—" she turned her dark graceful head away, "that man, Felicity. He's nice-looking in a way and I fell in love with him. It was three

123

years ago. I was still at school. I wrote him some mad letters and—then it died away and I never thought of it again except to think what an idiot I'd been and—I came across him again this year and he tried to start it again and, of course, I wasn't having any and—I found out quite by chance—he's told ever so many people about—it, only he pretends it's still lasting. He's shown lots of men the letters I wrote him—like an idiot, I didn't date them. Of course, father's rather well known now and—anyway, there he is showing my letters to any cad who'll look at them and talking as if I was still mad on him . . . Felicity, I didn't really mind at first. I thought it was too despicable to bother about, but now—now that Ronald's—well, now that this man's come here and might meet Ronald any day and show him the beastly letters I—oh, I can't *bear* it!"

"Ronald wouldn't listen," said Felicity.

"But I'd hate it," said Sheila. "I'd feel too ashamed to live."

Felicity remembered the time when she'd tried to get back some incriminating letters that didn't exist. She thought it rather kind of Fate to give her a chance of doing the real thing. And, of course, it wasn't only getting the letters back . . . Marmaduke Percival must meet his deserts. It was the duty of all decent people to see that he met his deserts.

"Sheila," she said slowly, "don't worry. I've got a plan."

When Felicity returned to the drawing-room, Lady Montague took her friend to see her pet plants in the conservatory, and Felicity was left alone with the poet. Very demure was Felicity, with shy, downcast eyes and softly-flushed cheeks. Marmaduke Percival looked at her—looked at her with interest. Never had Marmaduke Percival seen such vivid blue eyes, such black curling lashes, a mouth so like a sleeping child's, such glorious red-gold hair.

Felicity looked up and threw him a soft glance of admiration. Then she sighed and lowered her eyes again. Marmaduke Percival assumed his man-of-the-world manner.

"Well, little girl?" he said.

Felicity sighed again.

"Are you—interested in me?" said Marmaduke Percival kindly.

He was aware that this sounded slightly foolish, but somehow he did not think that this pretty child, who so evidently admired him, would find it foolish.

Felicity's eyes widened.

"Interested?" she said softly. "Oh, but interested's such a *weak* word . . . you're—you're so *wonderful!*"

She blushed and sighed and dropped her eyes. Marmaduke Percival could stand a lot of this sort of thing. He moved a little nearer her.

"Do you think so, little girl?" he said.

"Oh—*yes!*" breathed Felicity. He moved nearer still and, as is not the case with all girls, the nearer he was to her the lovelier Felicity looked.

"We're going to be great friends, little girl," said Marmaduke Percival.

Felicity clasped her hands.

"Oh!" she gasped. "*Friends!* . . . with *you!*—it seems too *wonderful!*"

For a moment Felicity was afraid that she'd laid it on a bit too thick, but her mind was soon set at rest. As a matter of fact, there was nothing in this line that Marmaduke Percival couldn't swallow. He moved yet nearer to her.

"We'll be *very* great friends, little girl," said Marmaduke Percival softly. "I'll teach you a lot of things," then added softly, as the door opened and Lady Montague and Mrs. Eltham returned, "Oh, damn!"

Lady Montague beamed upon them. "*So* nice for Felicity to know a *real* poet," she murmured. "Perhaps he'll be so very, very kind as to help her with her elocution. Her teacher says that she doesn't make *very* good progress."

Felicity answered demurely, long lashes lowered upon softly-flushed cheeks, "I think he's going to, aunt," she said.

People in the village never could agree afterwards as to who first suggested having a play to help the church funds. Quite a lot of people thought it was Felicity, and the people who didn't think it was Felicity thought it was themselves. Anyway, the idea was started, and in less than a day everyone had heard of it. A committee was elected (or elected itself) and Lady Montague was asked to be President. She invited the committee to tea at the Hall for the first meeting, and she also summoned Marmaduke Percival and his mother from The Grange.

"I've got the *very* person for a hero," she said mysteriously to the secretary of the committee.

The committee sat round the drawing-room of Bridgeways Hall, and with them sat the poet and his mother, and with them sat Felicity. The committee felt, as committees always felt in Lady Montague's presence, less like a committee than a small band of children who would soon be told what to do and who, till then, ought to be seen and not heard.

"Here's the hero," said Lady Montague, pointing dramatically and triumphantly to Marmaduke Percival. "Now, have you ever seen anyone more like a hero?"

The committee stared warily at Marmaduke as if they were afraid that he was going to go off like a bomb. Mrs. Eltham whispered to her neighbour, in a piercingly audible aside, "Marmy's *always* been handsome—he used to look *beautiful* in his little velvet suits." Marmaduke gazed into the distance and concentrated all his energies on looking beautiful and heroic, and Felicity threw him a glance of admiration which, in spite of his preoccupation, he did not miss.

"And now for the heroine," said Lady Montague.

"I propose Miss Felicity," said Marmaduke Percival promptly.

"Well," said Lady Montague doubtfully, "she's rather—*young*. Would you like to be the heroine, Felicity?"

"Yes, please," murmured Felicity demurely.

Then Moult came in with the tea and a buzz of conversation arose. Marmaduke Percival crossed over to the empty seat near Felicity.

"I'm—I'm so *thrilled*," murmured Felicity.

"We ought to rehearse soon," said Marmaduke.

126

Felicity raised her speedwell-blue eyes and looked at him through their heavy curling fringes.

"Let's rehearse to-morrow," she said. "Come here to rehearse to-morrow afternoon at three."

It wasn't till everyone had gone home that some of the more intelligent members of the committee realised that they hadn't yet fixed on a play . . .

Marmaduke Percival arrived very promptly the next afternoon. Felicity received him alone in the drawing-room.

"First of all," she said, "*do* read me your poems!"

Marmaduke had come not altogether unprepared for this request. He took the little book bound in white vellum from his pocket.

"Do sit just *there*," said Felicity.

"Why just here?" said Marmaduke.

"So that I can see you. You're so *handsome*," said Felicity, and added earnestly, "don't you *know* you're handsome?"

Marmaduke threw a complacent glance at his reflection in a hanging mirror.

"Well——" he said with a self-satisfied smile, "I suppose I am."

"Your *hair!*" said Felicity.

"Some people," said Marmaduke, "think I curl it, but I don't. It's quite natural."

"And your *eyes*."

Felicity was growing rather reckless, but she'd realised by this time what a lot of this sort of thing Marmaduke could swallow.

Marmaduke was still considering his own reflection with intense satisfaction.

"I must read you a letter a girl wrote to me once," he said. "She wrote a little poem about my eyes."

"Who?" said Felicity.

"That girl Sheila, who was here the other day." He gave a deep, deep sigh. "Poor girl! I'll tell you, because I'm sure you'll be sympathetic. I can't feel for her what the poor girl feels for me . . . It's always happening . . . That's the most trying part of having the misfortune to be out of the ordinary in looks.'

"*Do* read your poems to me," said Felicity.

He read in his little high-pitched voice for quite a long time. He read a poem "To a Flower Stalk," and another "To a Blade of Grass," and another "To a Drop of Rain," and another "To the Universe," and another "To a Fly Seen in Somebody's Soup." The last wasn't funny. At least it was, but it wasn't meant to be. And whenever he paused Felicity murmured "Wonderful!" or "Beautiful!" or "Marvellous!" or "Heavenly!" or simply "Oh!"

"Will you do something for me?" she said when he'd finished. Felicity was looking very, very lovely, so Marmaduke rashly said, "Anything," though, being a cautious man as far as regards doing services to other people, he qualified it afterwards by adding, "in reason."

"Write a poem for me," said Felicity.

He smiled.

"That's easily done," said Marmaduke, smiling. "What on?"

Felicity clasped slim brown hands.

"On yourself . . . I want one to remember you by . . . one always to bring your face to my mind—just look in the looking-glass and write one on yourself, will you?"

"Yes," said Marmaduke, "as a matter of fact, I've already written several, but I'll bring you one . . . anything else?"

"Yes . . . just little ones on all of us . . . on aunt, and on grandfather, and on all the people who were here the other day . . . the committee, you know . . . just so that I can always remember that day—the day when I first met you."

Marmaduke smiled.

"And bring them to me to-morrow, will you?" pleaded Felicity.

"Yes."

Then he went across to her.

"Felicity," he murmured amorously.

He meant to sit next to her on the settee and slip his arm round her waist. He thought he was doing it. But something went wrong somewhere. He must have slipped somehow. He found himself suddenly on the floor and Felicity right at the other end of the room, still smiling demurely, and watching him languishingly. He rose slowly to his feet.

Just then Lady Montague entered.

"We're rehearsing," said Felicity.

"Excellent!" said Lady Montague.

"I'm afraid I must go home now," said Marmaduke Percival.

He brought the poems the next day. "They're in the style of Walt Whitman," he said, "though I can't help thinking that I manage the thing a little better than poor old Walt did."

"You'll read them to me yourself, won't you?" said Felicity ecstatically.

"If you like," said Marmaduke kindly.

"And sit just here, *just* here," said Felicity, She seemed rather urgent upon the point. "So that I can see you better," she explained, "and read *loud,* please, because I'm just a little deaf to-day," she added unblushingly.

Clear to squeakiness, slow, distinct, came the voice of Marmaduke Percival reading aloud his poems. Felicity sat and listened with a far-away look in her eyes and a smile of satisfaction on her lips. The poems surpassed her wildest expectations . . .

She rose when he had finished.

"But how *lovely!*" she said, rising and going over to the fireplace. He went to her, slipped his arm round her waist, moved his head forward to hers and—most extraordinary—there he was on the floor again! Must have slipped on a footstool or something. And there was Felicity at the door looking back at him with a mischievous smile.

"So sorry I have to go," she murmured. "Aunt will give you tea . . . You won't forget there's a committee meeting about the play to-morrow, will you?"

Ronald came the next day. He came in reply to an urgent letter from Felicity. He brought with him an enormous box of chocolates for Felicity. Ronald, as a brother, was very satisfactory.

"Well, kid," he said, smiling down at her from his six-foot-six, "what's it all about?"

"Come up to the schoolroom," said Felicity, "and I'll tell you quietly . . ."

So they went to the schoolroom, which was now Felicity's own domain, and he sat on the table and lit his pipe, and said:

"Choke it up, kid. You're in some sort of a scrape, I suppose, and want me to get you out."

She laughed and picked out the most exciting-looking chocolate.

"Would you if I were?" she said, digging her firm, white teeth into it, and added, "Oh, *scrummy!* It's a strawberry sort of thing!"

"I'd do my damnedest to," he said determinedly.

Felicity finished the strawberry sort of thing, then she said, "You're a dear, Ronnie, but it's not my scrape this time."

She told him, watching his brow contract and his mouth tighten as she did so.

"Now, don't do anything *rash*, Ron," she cautioned him. "He's coming this afternoon for the meeting. You can have him *after* the meeting, but I want him *at* the meeting, please."

The meeting seemed doomed from the first. For one thing Sir Digby turned up, and that disconcerted everyone. Sir Digby felt well enough to get up and come downstairs, so he got up and came downstairs. And he was infuriated to find his drawing-room full of people he didn't know and didn't want to know. Of course, he could have made it more comfortable for everyone by going to sit in the library, but he wasn't in a mood to want to make it more comfortable for everyone. So he growled at them all as a preliminary greeting, then went to sit all by himself by the fire, reading a newspaper and growling again ferociously at intervals. An atmosphere of nervousness began to overspread the meeting. Marmaduke Percival, however, was quite unaffected by it. He divided his attention equally between his reflection in the mirror on the wall and Felicity's face. The expression on Felicity's face was somehow less satisfying than usual, so he concentrated on the reflection of his own, bestowing little caressing touches on his tie and his hair. The atmosphere of nervousness increased. Remarks on the weather died away, killed by Sir Digby's subterranean growls. Conversation languished. And three or four members of the committee were still absent, so that formal proceedings could not yet begin.

"Felicity," said Lady Montague, with the brightness of despair, "suppose you recite to us, dear, till the others come. One of those beautiful little poems that Mrs. Graves teaches you."

"Well," said Felicity, "I've got Mrs. Graves' phonograph here and—and it will recite *ever* so much better than I could. It will recite some *real* poetry to you."

Felicity did something to something hidden behind the palm where Marmaduke had sat the day before and immediately, to everyone's amazement, Marmaduke Percival's voice—high, squeaky, unmistakably Marmaduke Percival's—filled the room. Sir Digby was so much astonished that temporarily he forgot to growl.

"To myself," said Marmaduke Percival's voice.

> "I look in the mirror,
> What do I see?

I see a face that a Greek god might envy;
Hyacinthine locks,
Eyes fringed with thick black lashes.
A mouth like to a cherry or a rose,
Teeth of the purest whiteness and regularity.

> Beautiful, beautiful ears,
> Beautiful, beautiful nose.

A chin—no words could express the beauty of my chin. And I gaze and gaze at myself and cannot take my eyes away from myself.

> Because I am so beautiful."

A dull red had crept over Marmaduke's classic countenance. His midnight-blue eyes were darting hither and thither as if in search of escape. Sir Digby, his eyes almost starting out of his head, was listening enthralled. Upon everyone's face was blank open-mouthed amazement. Except upon Felicity's. Felicity sat, her eyes fixed demurely upon the ground, a faint mischievous smile upon her lips.

The instrument proceeded: "To Mrs. Harvey."

"When I see Mrs. Harvey, what do I think of?
I think of a balloon so inflated that surely it must burst soon.
I think of a great, large pale pudding.
With currant-like eyes. . . ."

Mrs. Harvey turned her currant-like eyes upon the poet. The eyes were more like forked-lightning than currants at the moment. Perspiration stood out upon the poet's brow. He breathed painfully. But no one spoke. Everyone was too much amazed to speak. A spell seemed to be upon them all. The voice continued: "To Lady Montague."

"How can anyone look at her without laughing?
    She is pompous and overfed.
    She has dyed hair and her chins are too numerous to count.
    She is hideously ugly, and I detest ugly things.
    So I detest her."

A sound came from Lady Montague that might have been a dying moan of agony or a cry for vengeance. The poet put his hand to his throat as though he found his collar too tight. And still no one moved. And still Felicity smiled demurely at the floor. And the voice went on: "To Sir Digby Harborough."

"Like a volcano is Sir Digby—
    An ugly volcano belching forth words of anger and fury.
    Unlovely to behold, like an apoplectic ape."

Providence at this moment restored to Sir Digby the power of speech. The volcano proceeded to belch forth words of such anger and fury that the poet, his face white as paper and his perfect teeth chattering with terror, rose and fled from the room.

But that wasn't all. Oh, no, that wasn't nearly all. For Ronald was waiting for the poet in the garden. And Ronald set to work with a will upon the beautiful, beautiful nose . . . And when Ronald had finished with him the Greek god wouldn't have envied his face any more.

When Felicity joined them in the garden Marmaduke Percival was lying on the ground propped up against a tree, and Ronald stood over him.

"He's shamming a faint," said Ronald, "he's only had a quarter of what he deserves."

"I don't like fighting," moaned the poet. "It's low and brutal and ugly and violent. I like everything that is beautiful. I don't like fighting."

"Felicity," said Ronald, "did the swine ever try to kiss you?"

"Yes, he *tried*," said Felicity.

"I kept falling over things," murmured the poet.

"That settles it," said Ronald. "Felicity, go and fetch my shaving things."

"If you cut my throat," said the poet, "you'll get hung."

But Ronald didn't cut his throat. Ronald shaved his head. Ronald shaved off all his hyacinthine locks till his head looked like a billiard-ball. He cut off the hyacinthine locks with a pair of scissors, then moistened his shaving-brush in the ornamental fountain just near, got a lovely lather, and shaved him clean. Ronald surveyed his handiwork critically.

"Now let him look at himself, Felicity," he said.

Felicity held out a hand-glass. Marmaduke gave one look at himself and then, with the cry of a stricken deer, fled into the night.

"That's *that!*" said Ronald with a deep, deep sigh of satisfaction." And I got the letters out of him, too. He'd got them in his pocket. Here they are. Go and burn them, there's a good girl."

They returned to the drawing-room. Sir Digby had retired to his own room. Lady Montague, still purple in the face, had taken the chair.

"I propose," she said, with majestic displeasure, "that Mr. Eltham shall *not* be the hero of this play."

There was a murmur of assent.

"Ronald," said Lady Montague, looking up at him as he entered, "will you be the hero?"

"Who's the heroine?" said Ronald cautiously.

"Felicity."

"No," said Felicity, "I've changed my mind. I'm not going to be. I propose Sheila."

"But does Sheila want to be?" said Lady Montague.

"I'll go and ask her," said Ronald. "I'll go and ask her now."

The Elthams left The Grange early the next morning.

The committee didn't manage to decide on a play after all.

But Ronald and Sheila met regularly just to practise the art of being hero and heroine, and got on very nicely with it . . .

Chapter Nine

Felicity Makes Amends

It was, of course, Felicity's familiar demon of mischief that inspired her to impersonate a Russian refugee, when Mr. Mellor called to see her grandfather. Mr. Mellor was one of her grandfather's friends, and a frequent visitor at the Hall. He was a little precise man—shortsighted and very absent-minded. Like Sir Digby, he was a collector, and they enjoyed comparing notes. They had a tacit arrangement by which Sir Digby listened to Mr. Mellor talking about his finds, and then Mr. Mellor listened to Sir Digby talking about his finds. And as soon as Sir Digby had finished with his finds Mr. Mellor got in again with his old finds. And so on. They spent some very happy hours together. But to-day Sir Digby was in bed with an especially bad attack of gout and was seeing only Wakeman, who had filled an entire note-book with new names and was feeling cheered and invigorated. For almost a month Sir Digby hadn't had a single bad day. For almost a month he had been uniformly polite and considerate to Wakeman. And Wakeman had been growing more and more taciturn and dejected. To-day, however, had made a new man of him. The zest of life had returned to him. His eyes shone. He moved about briskly and alertly. He had need, of course, to move about briskly and alertly, because already Sir Digby had thrown a footstool at him . . .

Lady Montague did not visit the Hall while Sir Digby was having a bad day. She stayed in the safe retreat of the Dower House until she heard that the worst was over.

Franklin was busy as usual. Sir Digby's morning post contained letters from fellow collectors all over the world, and all these had to be answered in detail, Franklin's knowledge of old manuscripts was by now almost as great as his employer's.

And Felicity was bored.

She saw the visitor coming up the drive from her bedroom window and her boredom increased. She'd have to give him tea. She'd have to listen to him for hours and hours and hours about his collection. Sir Digby's not being there -never made any difference. He didn't mind whom he talked to. He'd been to the Hall several times before this and found Sir Digby ill or out, and Felicity knew what it was like. He'd just talk and talk and talk and talk about his collection till she was so bored that she wanted to scream.

And suddenly she thought of the Russian refugee. She'd been to Sheila's for the week-end and they'd had charades and she'd dressed up as an old woman with a terrible wig and bonnet and a long black cloak—as much like Miss Smythe-Bruce as she could—and pretended to talk Russian.

That was how Mr. Mellor found her when he was announced a few minutes later. Fortunately for Felicity, he'd been round the garden to consult Drewe about a blight that was appearing on some of his chrysanthemums, and so had given her time to change. She was quite ready for him—fusty cloak, fusty bonnet, fusty veil, grey wig and everything. She explained, in very broken English, that she was an old friend of Lady Montague's who had been driven out of Russia by the Bolshevists. Then she began to talk Russian. First she talked plaintively, almost tearfully, then she talked earnestly, then she talked fiercely. He didn't, of course, understand what she said. Felicity was rather good at talking imitation foreign languages. She could put very deep feeling into her voice and the words she said, though they belonged to no language at all, always sounded convincing. An expression of horror descended upon Mr. Mellor's small precise face. He looked as if in the throes of a nightmare. When she grew tearful he looked desperately about him and mopped his brow. When she grew fierce he trembled. When she paused, as if for reply, he murmured "Quite," or "Exactly," or "Of course," in a voice that quivered with apprehension. He was clearly terrified. He didn't once mention his collection. He didn't, it was obvious, once think of his china. The trick came off perfectly. Felicity's familiar spirit of mischief danced an exultant dance in her heart. Franklin limped in to tea. He recognised her, but he played up to her. And after tea Wakeman brought a message that Sir Digby was better and would like to see Mr. Mellor. Gloom was evidently descending over Wakeman again. The worst was over. Sir Digby was no longer growling and throwing things. He was becoming apologetic and polite. All the zest was gone from life for Wakeman till the next bad attack.

Mr. Mellor crept thankfully from the room, keeping an apprehensive eye upon Felicity.

When he had gone Felicity whipped off the hat and veil and wig.

"Frankie, wasn't it fun?" she said.

"It was," he said, laughing, "but——"

"But what?" she said.

"I can't help laughing, Pins, but, honestly, you know, it wasn't cricket."

"What do you mean?"

"Well, you were in the position of hostess and he was your guest. Playing tricks on people in those circumstances isn't done. It puts them at a disadvantage." Felicity was silent for a minute, then she said slowly: "I see what you mean. I'll tell him, and apologise. I'd have done that anyway."

"Oh, don't worry about it," said Franklin cheerfully. "It doesn't really make any odds. I expect the poor chap needed a bit of excitement. It's probably done him good . . . I'd better go and see if Sir Digby wants me for anything now. So long, Pins."

Felicity went upstairs very thoughtfully. Frankie was right, of course. It hadn't been cricket. Felicity never rested satisfied under a sense of penitence and self reproach. Amends had to be made before Felicity's self-respect was restored to her.

Mr. Mellor was in the library talking to Franklin when she came downstairs again.

"It was me all the time," she said to him. "I was just playing a trick on you. I'm awfully sorry."

He laughed, and seemed rather relieved.

"You did it very well," he said, "I'm very glad it was you because, to tell the truth, I was feeling rather nervous. Where did you learn Russian?"

"It wasn't Russian," said Felicity simply. "It was just nothing."

"It was most convincing," he said. "*Most* convincing . . . Now what do you think of that?"

He pointed to a vase that stood on the desk where Franklin sat.

"I don't think much of it," said Felicity frankly, "do you?"

He looked rather shocked.

"My dear child, it's a very old and very rare piece of Sevres. I brought it to show Sir Digby. There should be a pair of them. It's got a fellow. If I could get the other fellow they'd be the gem of my collection."

"I suppose, now, you'll set off and hunt the whole wide world till you find its fellow," said Felicity.

Mr. Mellow sighed.

"It's much more complicated than that, my child," he said, "I've found the fellow. It belongs to a Mr. Percival Hunter, who's just come to live at Fairdene—not four miles away from here."

"And won't he let you have it if he knows you want it to make the pair?" said Felicity.

He smiled rather sadly.

"I'm afraid not. You see he's in the same boat. He wants mine to make a pair just as badly as I want his to make a pair."

"I see," said Felicity, "it is rather awkward, isn't it . . . Do you want it frightfully?"

"Yes," he admitted, "I do."

"More than anything else in the world?" said Felicity.

"It sounds childish," said Mr. Mellor deprecatingly, "but—but I do."

Then he packed up his vase, complimented Felicity once more on her Russian, and went home.

"Now, Pins," said Franklin, as soon as he had gone, "don't, for Heaven's sake, go and pinch Hunter's vase for Mellor just to make up for having pulled his leg. You'll land us all into trouble if you do."

"You have an almost uncanny power of reading one's more secret thoughts, Frankie," said Felicity, "but I'm not going to pinch anything of anyone's. I'm a law-abiding citizen."

Felicity had arranged to spend the next day with Sheila. She set off soon after breakfast. But before she set off she rang up Sheila.

"Sheila, darling, I'm afraid I can't come to-day, after all. May I come to-morrow instead?"

"*Oh!*" said Sheila, disappointed, "I'm *so* sorry, Pins. I *did* want you to-day—but I'll have to make the best of it. Why can't you come to-day?"

"To-day," said Felicity, "I'm setting forth on a very private and delicate mission. I may succeed and I may not. I'll tell you all about it to-morrow, anyway. But the point is that *officially* I'm spending the day with you. Don't tell anyone here that I'm not . . . Good-bye."

It was three and a half miles to Fairdene. It seemed shorter than that to Felicity because she'd got such a lot to think about. She'd got all the money she possessed (three pounds) in her pocket, and she was inventing little speeches in which she offered to pay Mr. Hunter three pounds now and five shillings a month out of her allowance for the rest of her life if only he'd let her have the vase. As a matter of fact, she didn't feel very confident. Somehow she couldn't imagine him handing over the vase in return for her three pounds now and a promise of five shillings a month for life. Probably Mr. Mellor had already offered him far more than that. Still—Fate might just possibly be on her side. Felicity always believed in giving Fate a sporting chance . . .

She'd reached Fairdene now and was walking slowly up the drive. A little of her courage had deserted her, but she whipped up the remnant and knocked loudly at the front door. There was no answer. She knocked again. Still there was no answer . . . They must be all out, thought Felicity. And yet somehow it didn't look like a house that was shut up and vacant of inhabitants. She knocked again and waited for several minutes. Still no answer.

Reluctantly she prepared to depart. She walked away from the door and past the French window of a room that was evidently a library. She glanced in and there a curious spectacle met her eyes. A man was crouching under a sofa by the wall. She could see his boots sticking out quite plainly. In an instant she made up her mind. The family was away, the house locked up, and this was a burglar who had been disturbed at his nefarious work by her knocking at the front door and was trying to hide under the sofa until the coast was clear again. Felicity's spirits rose. Though she couldn't get back the vase, at least she could capture a burglar single-handed. She'd always wanted to capture a burglar single-handed. She opened the French window and entered the room.

"Who are you?" she said sternly, "and what are you doing there?"

The man came out from under the sofa. He was a youngish man—tall and pale and frightened-looking.

"I'm—er—Mr. Hunter," he said, mopping his brow, "I live here. Who are you?"

Felicity was slightly taken aback, but she answered calmly.

"I'm Felicity Harborough. I've just been knocking at your front door and couldn't make anyone hear."

"No," he panted, still mopping his brow, "I'm awfully sorry. I thought you were my aunt. I'm expecting my aunt. I—I told them not to answer the door."

"Why?" said Felicity with interest. "Don't you like your aunt?"

He shuddered.

"No, I don't. I hoped that if I hid and no one went to the door, and she didn't see anyone about——"

"She'd have seen your boots," said Felicity. "I could see then quite plainly from outside. They were sticking right out. That's why I came in. I thought you were a burglar."

"Could you see my boots?" he said with interest. "I thought they were under the sofa."

"No, they were sticking right out," said Felicity. "She'd have seen them through the window."

"Of course it was a silly idea altogether," said the young man gloomily. "She'd have come in somehow whatever I'd done. As a matter of fact the door wasn't even locked."

"Why don't you like her?" said Felicity.

The young man groaned.

"You don't know what she's like," he said; "she's a tyrant. She's Mussolini and Judge Jeffreys and Bluebeard and Lenin and Nero and Lucrezia Borgia all rolled into one. She's—indescribable. She's been abroad for four years. They've been the happiest years of my life. But I heard from her this morning that she'd got back and was coming to make her home with me for a few months. It was, of course, in the wildness of despair that I pretended that I'd gone away and the house was empty. It wouldn't have been the slightest good. She'd have got in within five minutes. She'd have—Oh, Lord——!"

A taxi laden with luggage had drawn up at the door, and from it was descending a tall and excessively sternlooking woman carrying a Pom. The taxi man began to take the luggage down. The woman looked about her, saw the open French window and entered.

"Well, Percy," she said, "how are you?" She sniffed the air like an old war-horse. 'You've been smoking in this room. Now, please remember, that while I am staying with you there is to be no smoking in the house at all. You may smoke, if you wish to indulge in such a filthy habit, in the garden or in the tool shed. Not in the house. Not in any part of the house. Please remember that." Her eye bored him like a gimlet. He quailed before it. She turned to Felicity. "This is my secretary, I suppose. How long have you been here?"

"Only a few minutes," said Felicity demurely.

"There must have been a mistake. I told them not to send you till to-morrow morning. But, still, it doesn't matter much. I shall find plenty for you to do." She turned back to Percy who was still mopping his brow. "I wrote to the local registry office," she said, "and asked them to send me a young woman secretary here for the duration of my visit to you. They have sent her a day earlier than I engaged her, but, as I said, no matter. I shall find plenty for her to do." Her gimlet eyes flashed back to Felicity. "I don't know what your name is. I can't be bothered with people's names. I shall call you 'Harriet.' I always call my secretaries 'Harriet.' It saves trouble. Your duties will be to attend to my correspondence. I am secretary of a Total Abstinence Society, and an Anti-Swearing Society, and an Anti-Smoking Society, and an Anti-Dancing Society, and there is a good deal of correspondence connected with each. In fact, I've brought with me an attache case full of letters which you may start on at once.

"Then you will have to look after my little doggie here, Lulu. She is very sensitive and highly strung." As if to prove this, Lulu began to whine plaintively. "I shall want you to brush and comb her coat every morning —very gently, of course—and see that her roast chicken is tender at breakfast, lunch and dinner, and carry her about for me. Walking tires her. And you must always be within call to do any other little duties that I may require of you. Now go and take off your hat and coat. You'll begin your duties directly after lunch. We will lunch at one o'clock prompt, Percy, during my visit, please, and I shall want perfect silence during the afternoons, as I work and rest then. I do not like gramophones or loud-speakers in the house at all, and I must ask you not to entertain any of your friends here during my visit."

"Er—how long will your visit last, aunt?" quailed Percy.

"For four months, at any rate. If the place suits me I may stay for longer. I can see, my poor boy, that you need a woman's care. I feel that I have a duty to you, and I have never yet been known to shirk my duty. I will now go and prepare for lunch."

She swept out.

Percy turned to Felicity and mopped his brow again. "I—I am awake, aren't I?" he said. "It—it isn't a ghastly nightmare?"

"Yes, you're awake," said Felicity quite cheerfully; "it isn't a nightmare, though it certainly *is* rather ghastly."

He looked at her with sudden interest.

"I say," he said, "you—you aren't *really* her secretary, are you?"

"Why shouldn't I be?" challenged Felicity.

"You—you sort of don't look like a secretary," he said.

But the lunch bell rang, and with a, "Come along, she'll be mad if we're late," Percy drew her to the dining-room.

Percy's aunt was already in her place and Lulu was on the hearthrug.

"Miss Lulu," Percy's aunt was saying to the butler, "has chicken for every meal, and do not bring her anything but *breast,* please, lightly roasted and very tender. She cannot eat any part of the bird but the breast."

Lulu, asthmatic, corpulent, dyspeptic, and generally revolting-looking, turned her bleary eyes upon her mistress and emitted a nasal sound indicative of assent.

Percy's aunt then turned again to the butler and pointed sternly to the bottle that stood by Percy's glass.

"Remove that," she said sternly, "only water is to be drunk in this house during my visit." Percy made as if to protest, then met once more her gimlet eye and quailed beneath it. The butler hesitated, then, in his turn, met the gimlet eye and quailed beneath it. He removed the bottle. The gimlet eye had not finished with him. "Kindly bring me the key of the wine cellar directly after lunch. I am, as I think I said before, the secretary of a total abstinence society and, as such, I owe a duty to the community."

Percy wore a look of abject despair, Felicity looked her demurest, Lulu was already eating her chicken greedily and with a great deal of noise on the hearthrug. Percy's aunt continued: "During my stay here, Percy, I should like you and all the rest of the household to retire to bed at nine-thirty. I always retire to bed at that hour myself, and the slightest sound disturbs me, so that I find the only way of ensuring my night's rest is to insist—*insist* on everyone else in the house retiring at the same hour as I retire myself." Again Percy made as if to protest. Again he met the gimlet eye and relapsed into abjectness. She turned to the butler. "Give Miss Lulu a little more gravy, please. Don't you see that she's finished it?" The average funeral tea is far more cheerful than was the rest of that meal, but it came to an end at last, and Percy's aunt swept Felicity with her into the drawing-room.

"I intend to make this room my working-room during my stay

here, Harriet," she said, "and you will use the smaller drawing-room, so that you will be within call." The smaller drawing-room opened out from the larger drawing-room by an archway. A screen drawn across the archway in the larger drawing-room took the place of door or curtain.

"You will find a writing-table there," went on Percy's aunt. "You must be here by nine o'clock in the morning, ready to begin the morning's work. Is that quite clear?"

"Yes, thank you," said Felicity demurely.

Percy's aunt sat down, at the bureau, opened her attache case, and took out four or five little stacks of letters.

"You will wait now," she said, "while I make notes upon each as to the reply I wish sent and then you will take them into the other drawing-room and answer them. Meanwhile, please put Lulu on your knee. She prefers that to a cushion. Make her as comfortable as you can." Felicity gathered the wheezing little bundle of fur on to her knee. She was thinking hard. She hadn't forgotten the real object of her visit and she was still blindly trusting that fate would show her a way of obtaining it. The unspeakable Lulu was wobbling about on her knees trying to get comfortable, and Felicity was making her knees as bony as she could to prevent her. Suddenly Percy passed the open door on tip-toe. He was evidently going out for a walk, but did not wish to attract his aunt's attention. As he passed the open door he directed a furious grimace at Lulu. The effect upon Lulu was amazing. She leapt up snarling and trembling with anger. Her mistress turned to her in concern. She had not seen Percy pass the open door. She had only seen Lulu, seated upon Felicity's knee, display suddenly every symptom of apoplexy and hysteria.

"My poor darling," she said, "what is it? What happened then, pet? Tell missis, what was it?" Then, in her sternest manner, "What has upset her, Harriet?"

Felicity replied that she had no idea.

"Most strange," said Percy's aunt. "Really most strange. Quite suddenly, and for no apparent reason . . . but, of course, there must be *something*. *Something* must have upset her. She's so highly

143

strung—so responsive to atmosphere. So sensitive to the atmosphere of both places and people. She seems to have taken to you, Harriet, I'm glad to say. The letters are ready now. Put her on the sofa. On a cushion, of course. Make her *quite* comfortable. Put another cushion behind her back. Now go and answer the letters."

Felicity took the letters and went behind the screen through the archway and into the smaller drawing-room. She'd been much impressed by the effect of Percy's grimace upon Lulu. Surely, she thought, something could be made of it. She sat at the writing-table, her face cupped in her hands, thinking deeply. Surely something could be made of it . . .

And suddenly she remembered her face.

The select young ladies of Miss Barlow's very select school at Eastbourne frequently had unofficial face competitions, and the pupil who could produce the most horrible facial contortions won the prize. And Felicity always won it. Felicity's was not merely a face. It was a Face. Just as much as Felicity's normal natural face was the loveliest of all the normal natural faces at Minter House, so was her contortion of it the most hideous. Strong men blenched at the sight of Felicity's Face. Babies screamed at it. And so quickly could Felicity produce it and dispose of it that it had all the appearance of a hallucination. Those who saw it thought that it could never really have happened, that some strange and fleeting, waking nightmare must have come to them and gone in the fraction of a second.

But Felicity had not even practised her Face since her return from Minter House. The performance of it would have lacked zest without the stimulus of competition. Perhaps, she thought despondently, she'd lost the knack of it. A mirror hung over the writing-table. She tried it. Her spirits rose. She hadn't lost the knack of it. It was as perfect as ever. It was still the Face—unrivalled at Minter House throughout her whole career there.

She took up the letter on the top of the pile and glanced at the pencilled notes on it, then rose and went into the other room. Percy's aunt turned round from her bureau at once, yet in that first fraction of a second, before Percy's aunt's gimlet eyes had rested on her, Felicity had found time to fling a lightning Face at the now somnolent Lulu. The effect upon Lulu was again instantaneous and dynamic. Her somnolence departed, she snarled and whined, and yelped, and panted, and lashed herself into a wheezing, rasping, canine fury.

"Oh dear, oh dear," moaned Percy's aunt, "whatever's the matter? What is it, Lulu, my pet! There! There! What is it?"

"Perhaps my coming in suddenly disturbed her," suggested Felicity innocently.

"No, no. Of *course* it couldn't be that," snapped Percy's aunt irritably, "how *could* it be that? That couldn't *possibly* disturb her to this extent . . . I'm afraid it's the *atmosphere*. I told you before that she's very sensitive to atmosphere. I'm *afraid*," darkly, "that it's something in the atmosphere of the house that's upsetting her. Of course it may not be. It *may* be that, as you suggest, that she was dozing off and you disturbed her, but I don't *think* so. I've never known such a thing to affect her in that way, before . . . Are you better now, my pet?"

Her pet undoubtedly was. It was slobbering about on its cushion and settling itself again for slumber.

"What was it you wanted me for, Harriet?" said Percy's aunt majestically.

"I can't read this word," said Felicity, holding out the letter.

"It's perfectly plain," said Percy's aunt testily, writing it again more distinctly. "Do try not to bother me like this every other minute. Lulu must have absolute quiet."

Lulu's mistress was evidently feeling put out. She was losing her icy imperiousness and becoming snappy.

Felicity returned to the smaller drawing-room. She noted, with satisfaction, that the windows were low and opened on to the drive. At the first sight or sound of the real secretary, Felicity intended to be out of these window and down the drive like an arrow from a bow.

She sat at her desk for a few seconds in silence. Then she rose, flitted lightly and silently across to the archway, peeped round the screen, flung a Face at the blinking Lulu, then, like a flash and in less than a second, was back again at her desk.

Immediately Lulu had another seizure even worse than the last. She snarled and yelped, and panted, in a paroxysm of rage.

Percy's aunt wheeled round. She could just see, past the end of the screen, Felicity's red-gold head bent meekly over her work in the other room.

"Harriet," she called, "come at once, Lulu's having another attack."

Felicity came at once. They bent over the frantic Lulu and tried to soothe her.

"There, there then, pet," said Percy's aunt, "what is it, then? Tell missis."

While Felicity rearranged the cushions under Percy's aunt's direction.

Roast chicken in unlimited quantities has an atrophying effect upon the brain and Lulu was very stupid, because she never connected Felicity's face with Felicity's Face. She boiled with fury and indignation at the memory of that Face round the screen and then gazed with maudlin self-pity at Felicity's face hovering above her.

"It *couldn't* have been you coming in this time," said Percy's aunt, distracted. "Oh, it couldn't possibly, because you were at your desk writing the whole time, I saw you. I'm terribly, *terribly* afraid that it's the atmosphere of this house . . . She's calmer now. If we leave her she may sleep. She is very highly strung. She lives on her nerves. Simply *lives* on them. Well, you'd better go back to the correspondence, Harriet. Be as quiet as you can, of course. Lulu needs *absolute* quiet for her nerves. I fear they must be frayed to ribbons by these terrible, terrible attacks."

Felicity returned to the small drawing-room and sat down at the writing-table. Percy's aunt turned back to her bureau. Lulu lay on her cushion and panted asthmatically. Drowsiness overcame her. Her eyes blinked.

Then, suddenly—it came again.

The Face flashed round her side of the screen and as suddenly disappeared.

Her drowsiness vanished. She burst at once into a frenzy, howling, snarling, whining, and yapping, yelping and wheezing in an impotent transport of rage. Percy's aunt had turned round almost immediately. Behind the screen, in the next room, she could see Felicity's red-gold head still bent meekly over the writing-table. She was too far away, of course, to notice that Felicity looked a little breathless. She flew to the sofa side of her pet.

"What is it, then, Lulu darling?" she said again. "Tell missis."

Lulu proceeded to tell missis. She told Felicity, too (who had approached more slowly), all about the Face. She cursed the Face. She defied the Face. She snarled and barked, and raged at the memory of the Face.

"You see," said Percy's aunt to Felicity, with a gesture of despair, "it's an even worse attack than the previous one. It's *ruining* her nervous system. Her suffering's terrible to witness, isn't it? I'm convinced that it's the atmosphere of the house—the *moral* atmosphere, I mean. Dear Lulu's always so sensitive to that. There wasn't a sound to disturb her. Neither of us moved. It couldn't be anything but just the atmosphere. It's wearing her out. A day of this would kill her. I can't bear to watch her suffering in this way. I've no right to *expose* her to Such suffering. I've a duty to Percy, but I've a still greater duty to Lulu. I should never forgive myself, never, if in my desire to fulfil my duty to Percy I put a greater strain upon Lulu's nervous system than it can bear . . . No, I've made up my mind quite firmly. If Lulu has one more attack of this sort I leave this house for ever!"

And Lulu had one more attack of this sort. She had it before five minutes were out. It was even worse than the last. Percy's aunt gathered her into her arms—snarls and growls and whines, and all—and turned dramatically to Felicity.

"Kindly summon my nephew," she said.

"I think he's gone out for a walk," said Felicity.

"I can't wait for his return. I can't wait for his return. Every second is precious. Another attack may come on any second, and

147

she has no reserve strength to resist it . . . I will pack again at once and leave by the next train. Kindly order me a taxi. You may return to the registry office and tell them that I did not need you after all. I shall certainly not pay you for the little work you have done. In fact, I can't see that you have done any at all. You are slow and incompetent . . . if I am gone when my nephew returns from his walk tell him that I have left his roof because my innocent Lulu could not breathe its atmosphere. He may, or he may not, know why," she ended darkly, as she swept from the room. Percy returned an hour later.

Felicity was in the hall.

"What an age you've been," she said.

He still looked white and stricken. He glanced round fearfully and whispered.

"Where is she?"

"She's gone away," said Felicity, "for good."

He was amazed and incredulous.

"No!" he gasped.

"Yes," said Felicity calmly, "she's gone because her innocent Lulu cannot breathe the atmosphere Of your roof. You may, or may not, know why."

He sat down heavily on the neatest chair.

"She's—she's actually *gone?*"

"She's actually gone."

"It's—too good to be true."

"It is true."

"B-but—w-why did she go?"

"She went because I made my Face at Lulu."

"You made——" he gasped, bewildered.

Felicity flung him a Face.

So fleeting was it that it seemed hardly to have disturbed the exquisite repose of her faultless features, and yet—the young man blenched.

"Yes," said Felicity calmly, "that's how Lulu felt about it. That's why she went away."

He became rather thoughtful, and then said:

"I wonder how old Lulu is. What's the average life of a Pom? Do you know?"

"No, why?"

"I mean, I suppose I'm safe till Lulu dies and then she'll come back."

Felicity shook her head determinedly. "No, she won't. Don't you worry. She'll never come back to the roof whose atmosphere caused her little Lulu such terrible nervous suffering. Never. She'll owe that to Lulu's memory."

He grinned.

"I can hardly believe it, yet," he said; "it seems too good to be true . . . I've spent all this afternoon wondering which form of suicide was least painful."

"They're all nasty," said Felicity, "and they all just mightn't come off, and then you'd feel such a fool."

The postman appeared suddenly at the open front door. Percy went to him and absently took the post-card he held out.

"It's to my aunt," he said to Felicity. "I'd better forward it, but I don't know where she's gone . . . it's from a registry office."

"Let me look at it," said Felicity, taking it from him, "I shouldn't bother to forward it. It's only to tell her that they can't send her a secretary."

"Then you, then you *aren't* a secretary," he gasped.

"Of course not," said Felicity. "I can't spell for nuts and I always got four marks taken off for bad writing at Minter House. It generally left me none at all."

"Then what—why—what did you come for?"

"I came about your vase."

"My vase?"

"Yes, you've got an old Sevres vase, haven't you?" He considered for a moment, then said dreamily:

"Yes, I have . . . It's a very curious thing . . . This morning—it seems years and years and years ago—I've lived through so much since then—this morning I was as keen as nuts on that vase. I was thinking of nothing but how to get its fellow from a man who I know has got it. . . . Isn't it funny what a lot of difference a day can make to one's outlook on life. To-day I've looked on the—er—naked face of horror."

"Do you mean my Face?" said Felicity with pride.

"No," he said, "I mean my aunt's and Lulu's. I've come face to face with reality. I've seen the cup of life dashed from my lips and then miraculously raised to it again, and all that sort of thing. That vase seems to belong to a different world, in a different life. It seems amazing that this morning I was thinking of nothing else, but—but—but what *did* you come here for?"

"I came for the vase," said Felicity simply. "'I was going to offer you three pounds for it and five shillings out of my allowance for as long as you'd like."

"But I'll *give* it you," said the young man eagerly, "I *want* to give it you. I'd *like* to give it you. You've saved me from—from—well, you've seen my aunt and Lulu. You know what you've saved me from. Take the vase and everything else you like. I'll give you the whole bally house, if you like."

"I don't want the whole bally house, thank you very much," said Felicity politely, "but I *should* like the vase, if you really feel like that."

"I *do*," protested Percy. "I couldn't possibly tell you how much I feel like that. I'm just glad that there's something I *can* give you. I'd never sleep a wink till I'd done something to prove my gratitude, anyway."

"Well, I'd hate you to do that," said Felicity, "and I really do want the vase for a friend of mine. But I'm perfectly willing to pay what I can for it."

"Nonsense!" said Percy.

And he wrapped up the vase for her.

And she took it home.

It was dusk when she reached the Hall.

Franklin was limping across the hall.

"Hello, Pins," he greeted her cheerfully. "Had a jolly day with Sheila?"

"I've had an *awfully* jolly day," said Felicity happily, "but not with Sheila. I've not been to Sheila's."

"Haven't you? I thought that was the programme to-day."

"It was, but I altered it. I've been over to Fairdene." Proudly she unwrapped her parcel. "I've got the other vase for Mr. Mellor, Frankie, so it's all right now, isn't it?"

Chapter Ten

Mrs. Fanning's Psychic Experience

Ronald and Sheila were engaged.

Sheila was rapturously happy. There was only one cloud over her brightness.

"It's Daddy," she confided to Felicity. "I can't bear to think of leaving him. He does so hate doing things alone. It isn't," she added humbly, "that I'm intelligent or anything like that. He doesn't want that. He just wants someone to do things with. Gardening and walks. Walks are the things he likes doing most. And it isn't as if he wants someone to talk to. He's generally thinking out his book and doesn't want to talk. He just wants someone to be with him, and he feels—sort of lost and unhappy if no one's there. He doesn't enjoy his walks at all if he has to go alone."

"But—there's your aunt, isn't there?" said Felicity.

Sheila sighed.

"Have you met Aunt Hester?" she said.

"Not often," said Felicity. "She's generally not well, or lying down, when I've been to your house. But she seemed all right when I did see her."

"She's awfully nice," said Sheila. "If only——" she sighed again.

"If only what?" prompted Felicity.

"You see, she thinks she's an invalid," said Sheila. "She won't take any exercise. She won't even go out-of-doors. And she hardly eats anything at all. It'll be *horrid* for poor Daddy. She's perfectly well, really. All the doctors know that she's perfectly well, really, but if ever any of them dares to say so to her she simply stops having him and calls in someone else. It's just as bad as if she were a real invalid. Worse in a way. She'll be no company at all for poor Daddy when I'm married.

She's always weighing herself and, of course, she gets thinner and thinner with eating nothing and with never going out. She always feels tired and limp . . . It'll be *miserable* for Daddy with only her. I try not to feel worried about it, but I can't help it. And the pity of it is that really—*really*, if only she wouldn't imagine herself an invalid she'd be quite jolly."

"You're all coming to us next month, aren't you?" said Felicity, thoughtfully. "That might wake her up."

"It won't, said Sheila, gloomily, "it can't *possibly*. She'll eat nothing and lie down all day as usual. Your aunt, of course, will encourage her. People who belong to the Victorian age love chronic invalids. It was everyone's ambition in those days to be a chronic invalid. They adored them. And the next best thing to being a chronic invalid yourself was ministering to one. Oh, no . . . your aunt, I'm afraid, will only make things worse."

There were a good many people staying at Bridgeways Hall. Rosemary, of course, was there, and several of her friends—in particular, a dark and very handsome young man who was reputed to be enormously wealthy, and who was quite evidently deeply in love with her. Rosemary did not treat him any differently from her other admirers. She was, as usual, cold and distant and rather insolent, and yet Felicity suspected—she didn't know why—that she was going to accept him when he proposed. He was nice-looking, but there was something about his smile and about his eyes that Felicity didn't like.

"Do you like him, Rosemary?" she said tentatively, on one of the rare occasions when they were alone together.

"Whom?" drawled Rosemary.

"Sir Bertram."

"No," said Rosemary.

"I'm so glad," said Felicity, relieved.

"Why?"

"I'd been so afraid you were going to get engaged to him."

"I probably am," drawled Rosemary. "I hate all men, but that's no reason for not marrying. I told you that once before, didn't I? He's rich. He's in love with me. He's probably as much a beast as any other man, but—well," she shrugged her shoulders, "I've always told you that I was going to marry a rich man. It might as well be he as any other. It will be quite a fair bargain. I want money. He wants me. I'll get the worst of it probably, but the woman always gets the worst of it whatever she does."

Felicity shook her red-gold head firmly.

"I don't think that people or things are half as horrid as you make out they are," she said.

"Don't you?" said Rosemary. "Wait till you know a bit more of the world."

"I know a *lot* of the world," said Felicity with dignity, then she added wistfully, "Rosemary——"

"Yes?"

"You always seem, somehow, as if you were—were covering up your real nice self by an—unreal horrid self—as if—just because you'd met—perhaps one horrid person you were trying to make yourself believe that everyone was horrid—but I wish you wouldn't treat me like a baby, Rosemary. I wish you'd let me—help."

Rosemary looked down at Felicity's lovely wistful face, and suddenly her blue eyes lost their hardness.

"You're a darling, Felicity," she said. "It's *hateful* to think of your being let down by people and—finding out how *beastly* things are——"

Suddenly, as if by an illuminating vision, Felicity saw behind Rosemary's coldness and arrogance something sweet and trusting that had been hurt and had gone there to hide.

"Oh, Rosemary," she said eagerly. "I'm sure it isn't like that. I'm sure that people aren't——"

She stopped. Rosemary had drawn her defences of disdainfulness about her again. Her eyes were hard and mocking.

"What a very interesting conversation it is, isn't it?" she drawled, "but I'm afraid I haven't time to continue it. Good-bye, Infant."

And she went out.

Felicity bit her lip. It always made her angry when Rosemary called her "infant." And yet she couldn't really feel angry with Rosemary. There was something about Rosemary that made her heart ache with pity. But, still—she hadn't really much time or thought to spare for Rosemary.

She had other things to think of just now.

Sheila's aunt had arrived and Lady Montague, as Sheila had prophesied, was encouraging her. Lady Montague enjoyed ministering to a chronic invalid.

"Don't get up, dear, till tea-time," she would say every morning, "I know how *delicate* you are. You eat *nothing*, my dear, and you look *so* frail."

She seemed to take almost a personal pride in Mrs. Fanning's lack of appetite and pallor, as if in some way it lent distinction to the house-party.

For Mrs. Fanning, being continually informed with evident admiration by Lady Montague that she ate *nothing*, seemed to feel it incumbent upon her to eat nothing. She lay about on a sofa, all day, looking pale and eating nothing.

But Sheila hadn't very much time to worry about it, because Ronald was there and she couldn't really worry over anything with Ronald there. It was Felicity who worried.

For Mr. Partridge, Sheila's father, did seem a little lost and wistful. Sheila was always out with Ronald and he'd no one to go walks with and he hated having no one to go walks with. Felicity went with him whenever she could, but, of course, she couldn't always go with him.

She couldn't even tell Franklin why she was worried, because Franklin was just as he always was when Rosemary was at home—grim and tense, and silent, and looking older than he really was. He always looked wretched when Rosemary was in the house. And no wonder, thought Felicity indignantly. For Rosemary was hateful to him. It made Felicity go hot with shame to hear the way Rosemary spoke to him on those few occasions when she did speak to him. She was deliberately rude to him . . .

In fact, there were just now quite a lot of things in Felicity's world to worry her, but she was concentrating on Sheila's aunt.

Sheila's aunt came down for tea about a week after the beginning of her visit. She was, as usual, the perfect invalid—pale, fragile, drooping, dressed to suit the part in a clinging tea-gown. Lady Montague hovered about her like the priestess of some sacred rite—arranging her on the sofa, lowering her voice to ask her how she was, murmuring in hushed admiration, "No tea? Nothing to eat? My dear, how do you manage to keep alive at all?"

Felicity watched them with a little worried frown.

The conversation had turned on ghosts.

"Is Bridgeways Hall haunted?" Sheila was saying. "If it isn't, it ought to be."

"It is supposed to be," said Ronald carelessly. "The Lady Georgia Harborough, whose portrait is in the hall, is supposed to haunt it, but none of us have ever seen her."

Felicity noticed that a flicker of interest came over the invalid's face.

"Do tell me about it," she said breathlessly, "I'm so much interested in anything psychic."

But, of course, the drawback of having a faint, frail invalid's whisper is that often no one hears it, and as Lady Montague had now gone to the other end of the room no one heard Mrs. Fanning's remark except Felicity, who pretended not to have heard it, and the conversation drifted naturally from ghosts to beet-sugar and the government.

Then the party split up. Ronnie and Sheila went out to play tennis, Matthew and Marcia went out for a walk, Rosemary and Sir Bertram went into the morning-room, Sir Digby and Franklin and Mr. Mellor went into the library. Lady Montague went to interview the house keeper and Mr. Partridge went out for a walk by himself. He looked rather pathetically at Felicity before he went out. She knew that he wanted her to come with him, and so tender was Felicity's heart that it was very difficult to steel it against that look.

The door closed behind him.

She was left alone with Mrs. Fanning.

"Did you say," murmured Felicity softly, "that you were interested in psychic things?"

So eager was Mrs. Fanning that she quite forgot to use her invalid's whisper.

"Oh, *frightfully*, my dear," she said, "I had a book out of the library, just before I came away, I've forgotten what it was called, but it was full—*full* of authenticated cases of ghostly visitations and—er—messages and that sort of thing. Most extraordinary, and *all* authenticated. No room for doubt at all. You know, dear," she sunk her voice, "I've always been *convinced* that I'm psychic. I've never yet actually *seen* anything, but I've never ceased to hope. I can *feel* my psychic powers, though, as I told you, they have never yet been actually put to the test. But," she sank her voice to a yet more thrilling whisper, "I know people personally who've actually *seen* things."

"What have they seen?" said Felicity.

The invalid was sitting up on the couch, entirely forgetting her fragile droop.

"One of them—a friend of a friend of mine—was once staying in a house where an old treasure was supposed to have been buried for centuries, and in the middle of the night an apparition appeared, beckoned her out into the garden, and pointed to a certain spot, and told her to dig. This friend of my friend's dug, and what do you think she found?"

"What?" asked Felicity, obligingly.

"The treasure, my dear," said Mrs. Fanning impressively. "The treasure; wasn't it wonderful? I didn't know her personally, as I told you before, but my friend knew her—or rather it was, I believe, a friend of my friend's who knew her, but it's an absolutely authenticated case. And now, my dear, *do* tell me about the ghost that haunts this house."

During this recital Felicity's eyes had danced, then hidden themselves under their thick tawny lashes.

"Well, it's the most curious case," said Felicity slowly, "because it's almost the same as the one you just told me of—the buried treasure, you know."

"No, my dear," said Mrs. Fanning, deeply impressed. "*No! Do tell me!*"

"Well," went on Felicity, with a look of innocence in her eyes that would have put those who knew her on their guard. "It was a Lady Georgia Harborough, you know."

"Yes, yes . . . that was the name they said at tea. I remember."

"She was supposed to have hidden a treasure—no one knows exactly where—when she died, and she left a paper, saying that she would come back when the right time came and reveal its hiding-place."

"When the right time came," repeated Mrs. Fanning. "What did she mean by that?"

"I don't know," said Felicity.

"I expect she meant," said Mrs. Fanning eagerly, "when she could get into contact with anyone really psychic staying in the house."

"I expect so," said Felicity carelessly, "anyway, none of us have ever seen her. . . . Oh, and she also said in the paper she left that the person to whom she appeared to reveal the hiding-place of the treasure must find it herself—or himself, and mustn't breathe a word of her—er—visit, or else some evil would befall her—or him."

"How *interesting!*" said Mrs. Fanning. "How *wonderful!*"

"That's all I know about it," said Felicity carelessly. "You—er—you won't mention it to any of the others, will you? They don't like it mentioned. It—er—upsets them."

Mrs. Fanning nodded her head understandingly.

"Of course," she said, "people who aren't psychic generally *shrink* from such things. They're *repelled* by them. Now I, on the other hand, *am attracted*. The psychic always attracts me. I feel no shrinking at all from a visitant from another world."

"No," said Felicity soothingly, "but I'm sure you ought to rest now, oughtn't you?"

"Rest?" said Mrs. Fanning, then remembering that she was an invalid who found the slightest movement an effort and who could not raise her voice above a whisper, she sank back upon her sofa and said faintly, "Yes, dear child, you're right. I have been exerting myself too much. I will rest a little now."

Felicity crept away and left her.

She went to the morning-room, where Rosemary sat with Sir Bertram.

Sir Bertram was talking ardently, and Rosemary was working at a piece of tapestry and looking very beautiful and aloof.

"Rosemary," said Felicity, "will you lend me that Lady Georgia costume you had for the fancy dress dance?"

"What on earth do you want it for?"

"Oh, just to try on," said Felicity.

"If you like," said Rosemary. "Marie will tell you where it is. The wig's with it, too, I believe."

"Thanks, awfully," said Felicity.

She went out and met Mr. Partridge in the hall, just coming in from his walk.

"I'm so sorry I couldn't go with you," she said.

He smiled.

"It's foolish of me, isn't it?" he said, "to want company on my walks, because, as you know, I don't talk. It's just that I like to have someone with me and, of course, my sister isn't strong enough to walk. I shall miss Sheila *very* much indeed when she leaves me."

"Mrs. Fanning's health may improve," suggested Felicity brightly.

He shook his head.

"I doubt it," he said, "I very much doubt it."

The moonlight was pouring into Mrs. Fanning's room when she woke with a start and looked about her. She sat up in bed and stared at the open French window leading on to the balcony.

Her eyes opened wider, and wider, and wider, and wider.

There, at the window, in a shaft of moonlight, stood Lady Georgia Harborough, exactly as she was pictured in the portrait downstairs, the elaborately-dressed dark-brown hair, the white face, the billowing, flowered, silk dress.

A smile of rapture came to Mrs. Fanning's face.

At last the dearest wish of her heart was being gratified.

At last the dream of her life was being fulfilled.

At last she was having a psychic experience.

The visitant took a step forward, put up a white finger and beckoned—very slowly and impressively.

Without a word Mrs. Fanning got out of bed, put on a big coat and her shoes and stockings, and prepared to follow the ghostly visitant. The ghostly visitant led her out on to the balcony, down the fire-escape steps, and into the moonlit garden. It led her through the moonlit garden to a bed next to the kitchen garden, pointed to it, wrung its hands, then disappeared.

Mrs. Fanning looked about her. A spade stood conveniently near the bed. Mrs. Fanning seized this and set to work with a will.

She dug for two hours, but did not find any hidden treasure.

Then, still feeling thrilled and uplifted, despite her failure to locate the treasure, she went back to bed and fell at once into a dreamless sleep.

She awoke next morning aching in every limb and feeling very hungry.

When the maid came in with her usual breakfast— a pot of tea and a quarter of a slice of dry toast—she looked at it indignantly, and said:

"I'd like something more than this, please."

The maid looked surprised.

"You generally say this is too much, mum," she said, "shall I bring you an egg?"

"An egg *and* bacon, please," said Mrs Fanning very firmly.

She was so excited all that day that she could hardly wait for the night. After tea she said mysteriously to Felicity, "You remember what we were talking of yesterday afternoon?"

Felicity seemed to ponder deeply for some time, then, as if suddenly remembering, said, "Oh, yes, I remember."

"Well," confided Mrs. Fanning yet more mysteriously, "I'm having most wonderful, *wonderful* experiences, dear child. Psychic experiences. Wonderful. I can't tell you what they are, of course, and you mustn't even mention to anyone else that I'm having them. You'll promise me not to, won't you."

Felicity promised not to.

The next night Mrs. Fanning intended to slip out and continue her digging, but despite her determination to stay awake she fell asleep almost at once. As a matter of fact, she'd been feeling unusually sleepy all day. She had gone to lie down after lunch and had slept from two to four. It had been, too, with a certain wistfulness in voice and eyes that at tea-time she said, "No, thank you, dear," to Lady Montague's "Nothing to eat, I suppose, dear?"

She woke up with a start. Once more the ghostly visitor— elaborately-dressed brown hair, pale face, silk draperies, and all— stood in the shaft of moonlight, beckoning. Once more Mrs. Fanning rose, slipped on coat, stockings and shoes, and followed her down the stairs to the garden. And, this time, the ghostly visitant led her to a different part of the garden, pointed to quite a different bed, wrung her hands again, and again disappeared. There were several yew hedges about the garden—thick and tall—that were very convenient for disappearing. Mrs. Fanning seized the spade that lay near, and dug away in a sort of fine frenzy of inspiration. She was so stimulated and thrilled by the psychic experiences she was passing through that she felt no weariness at all. She could have dug for ever. She didn't find the buried treasure, but she still felt so excited by the memory of her ghostly visitant that she really didn't mind. She dug till the first streaks of dawn appeared, then retired to bed and fell into a heavy sleep—so heavy that she didn't feel at all ready to awaken when the maid appeared in the morning.

"Er—would you be wanting an egg and bacon this morning, mum?" said the maid rather nervously, "or just the dry toast."

"Two eggs and bacon, please," said Mrs. Fanning, very firmly. She wrote letters all morning, and she made quite a good lunch. She lay down all afternoon and she came down very promptly for tea.

"Nothing to eat for you, dear, I suppose, as usual?" said Lady

Montague, in the voice of hushed reverence in which she always said it.

And, to her great surprise, Mrs. Fanning said, rather snappily, "Yes, please, dear. The buttered toast. Thank you."

Sadly Lady Montague watched Mrs. Fanning eat two slices of buttered toast and half-a-dozen sandwiches. It was as if she had discovered her idol to have feet of clay. She had looked upon Mrs. Fanning as the one perfect lady of her acquaintance, and it was sad to see her fall thus from her high estate. Of course, it might be a symptom of some virulent disease. Lady Montague was, in fact, inclined to think that it must be that. Tentatively she said:

"Do you feel—ill at all, my dear?"

And instead of answering faintly, weakly, reproachfully, as she'd have answered a few days ago, "My dear, I *always* feel ill," she said, almost snappily, "Of course not. I feel perfectly well."

They all dispersed after tea, except Felicity. So, as Mrs. Fanning simply had to confide in someone, she confided in Felicity.

"Do you remember our little conversation the other day, dear?" she said, in a confidential whisper.

Felicity said that she did.

"Well—I can't tell you much, of course, but my psychic experiences are continuing, growing more and more wonderful. *Deeper* and more intimate. To describe them would be, of course, to betray the trust placed in me by the—er—psychic powers. But the most wonderful part of it all is, my child, the *healing* power it brings. Wonderful. Amazing. A curious sense of physical fitness to which I have always till now been a stranger."

Felicity, her thick lashes lowered over dancing eyes, forebore to remark that always till now Mrs. Fanning had been a stranger to good bouts of hard digging, lasting for several hours.

"Contact with the psychic world," went on Mrs. Fanning, "seems to bring with it the most amazing flow of—er—health and energy."

Felicity raised her eyes.

Mrs. Fanning's were fixed upon her intently. Felicity's met them with perlucid innocence.

"You're—not unlike the—er—Lady Georgia Harborough whose portrait is in the hall, are you, dear?" said Mrs. Fanning.

"No," said Felicity, still with perlucid innocence. "She was my ancestress, you know."

"Of course"—Mrs. Fanning was still studying her intently—"her hair is—I mean—was darker and she's—I mean—was much paler than you. Otherwise—in the features—there's a distinct resemblance."

"Do you think so?" said Felicity. "Do you think I'm very like her portrait?"

"Ah, no," said Mrs. Fanning mysteriously, "I wasn't thinking of the *portrait*. Not of the *portrait*. No, not the *portrait*. Ah!" she shook her forefinger playfully at Felicity, "you mustn't try to make me tell you things that I mustn't tell to anyone. Those who live in contact with the psychic world, dear, have *great* responsibilities, and one of them is silence in the presence of the uninitiated, dear, if you know what I mean, and I'm afraid that, psychically speaking, most people are uninitiated. Only to a very few of us is it given to pierce the veil. All I will say to you, dear, is that I'm going through experiences that I am sure you would love to share with me" (Felicity's mouth twitched for a second, then regained its wistful solemnity).

But, earnestly, "to change the subject, dear—where *exactly* is this treasure supposed to be?"

"No one knows," said Felicity, "she's supposed to come back to tell someone—you remember, I told you the other evening? . . . and that the others hate it being mentioned." Felicity spoke almost anxiously. She wanted to make that point *quite* clear, "and that if the one she appears to tells anyone some evil comes to her—or him."

Mrs Fanning gave a little amused laugh.

"Oh, my dear, you may trust *me* to keep my own counsel. You know, dear, I feel this night I am to enter upon a *deeper* stage of psychic revelation. . . . What a long time they are coming for the tea-things. Yes, dear, if you'll pass it, I'll have that last sandwich. I do so hate to see anything wasted."

*

Mrs. Fanning was right. That night she entered on a second, deeper stage of psychic revelation. The figure appeared as usual on the shaft of moonlight, stood silent and motionless for a few seconds as usual, then slowly beckoned. Mrs. Fanning had her coat and shoes ready by her bed, but this time the figure did not lead her down to the garden. It led her, instead, down the stairs to the hall. On the wall in the hall hung a large map of the surrounding district. The figure approached this, put out a white finger, touched a certain spot, and while Mrs. Fanning was eagerly bending her short sight upon the spot, disappeared. There was a leather screen just near the map that was very convenient for disappearing. Mrs. Fanning stood staring at the map. The figure had touched Frene Hill—a hill about four miles from the Hall. No one, thought Mrs. Fanning, not even a ghost, could expect her to trapse out there in the middle of the night with just a coat over her nightdress. She went slowly back to bed and fell asleep again. She woke up a little less hungry than on the preceding two mornings, and only had one egg with her bacon.

Someone enquired for her during the morning.

"I expect she's writing letters in the drawing-room," said Lady Montague.

But the drawing-room was empty except for Felicity, who was yawning over a book. Felicity felt rather sleepy these mornings.

"Then she's resting in her bedroom," said Lady Montague in tones of deep satisfaction, "she's a *perfect* invalid, you know," she added with pride. "Eats nothing. Never sleeps a wink at night, and has to rest all day. A perfect *martyr*."

But Mrs. Fanning wasn't resting in her bedroom. Mrs. Fanning, breathless and flushed with exercise, had just finished the four-mile walk to Frene Hill, and was borrowing a spade from a cottager. She then began to dig up the earth on the top of the hill. She worked vigorously. A small crowd of children gathered round to watch, but very little local interest was aroused. It was known that there was a house-party at the Hall and members of house-parties are notoriously mad.

She returned to the Hall in time for lunch.

She hadn't found the treasure, but in spite of that she felt much invigorated. She ate an enormous lunch. Lady Montague tried not to watch her eating an enormous lunch, but her eyes kept wandering to her in fascinated horror.

After lunch, she drew Rosemary on one side.

"That poor Mrs. Fanning!" she said, "I'm afraid it's the beginning of the end."

"What end?" said Rosemary, without much interest.

"Didn't you notice at lunch? Her hectic flush and feverish eyes."

"I noticed that she ate more than anyone," said Rosemary, indifferently.

"My dear, that's what I mean. It's the beginning of the end. She's been wasting for years. *Wasting*. Literally *wasting*. And then comes this sudden—er—abnormal appetite, this hectic flush, this feverish sparkle in the eyes. I only hope the end won't come when she's here. It would be so very awkward for us—with the house full of visitors. . . ."

But Rosemary wasn't interested, so she went off to try and find a more sympathetic audience. She found Felicity curled up on the window-seat of the morning-room, half asleep. Lady Montague did not often confide in Felicity, but to-day she had to confide in someone and there was no one else. Felicity gave her all the sympathy she could desire. Felicity, with demure blue eyes and fugitive dimples, agreed with all she said.

"I expect that at this very moment," ended Lady Montague, "the poor woman is lying on her bed trying to fight this last attack of the enemy. I will beg her to-night to call in a doctor."

But the poor woman wasn't lying on her bed trying to fight this last attack of the enemy. The poor woman was on Frene Hill again digging for all she was worth. She'd started off directly after lunch, found the walk a mere nothing, and set to work with vigour. She didn't find the treasure, but she didn't feel tired. In fact, she felt that she could have gone on digging during the whole evening if she hadn't been so frightfully hungry. She got back a little late for tea. Extraordinary, she thought, irritably, what wholly inadequate provision people made for tea nowadays. When all was said and done, it was a meal like any other meal, and at a meal one surely had a right to expect enough to eat. When Moult had been summoned three times to replenish the dish of buttered toast for her she began to notice that the other guests were looking at her rather pointedly, but the knowledge didn't trouble her at all. She was bathed in that delicious sense of weariness that only a day's hard exercise can bring. She wanted a good tea and she was going to have it, and then she was going to have a hot bath and a rest.

Lady Montague watched her in horror. She was realising that this was not the beginning of the end after all. The flush was the flush of rude health. The clear eyes were the clear eyes of rude health. The appetite was the appetite of rude health. Mrs. Fanning wasn't an invalid at all. She'd fallen with a crash from the pedestal upon which Lady Montague had set her, and never again did she ascend it. Ever after this day Lady Montague was cold and reserved in her manner to her. Ever after this day Lady Montague, when discussing her with other people, said, "Yes, she's very nice indeed, but——" This, of course, is by the way, because it never troubled Mrs. Fanning or anyone else.

Mrs. Fanning was very sleepy that evening and went to bed very early, but before she went she had another little conversation with Felicity. She called her on one side and said, in a confidential whisper, "I was right, dear. My—my psychic revelation did enter on a second and deeper stage last night. It's not as clear as it seemed to be at first. It's—it's not just a case of—the buried treasure, I think. I think there's some *deeper* meaning, after all. I can only follow and obey and the meaning will come to me sooner or later. But, my dear, I can't describe the feeling—the feeling of health and well-being that contact with the psychic world brings one. I can't tell you any—er—more detail, you know, dear, because as you told me yourself, one shouldn't. I'm very sleepy and I'm going to bed now, dear child, so I'll say good-night. I only hope that yet another psychic vision may be granted me."

Her wish was granted. Yet another psychic vision was granted her that night, and the night after, and the night after that. And, indeed, every night the psychic vision took her down to the hall and pointed out a spot on the local map several miles from the Hall, and disappeared while she was studying. And every morning Mrs. Fanning set off to this spot on the local map and dug there, and came home to lunch, and then went off there again, and dug there in the afternoon. She went in all weathers. Her face grew weather-beaten. Her eyes grew yet brighter. She ate enormous meals. Lady Montague could not look at her without wincing. In the end the psychic vision tired of it before Mrs. Fanning did. The dress and wig took a lot of arranging, and it was growing harder and harder every night to keep awake till the midnight hour beloved of ghosts. Moreover, the moon was waning and the whole thing was becoming less impressive without moonlight. So, at the end of the week, Felicity, finding Mrs. Fanning alone in the drawing-room, had another little conversation with her. She began brightly and naively.

"Do you remember my telling you about a fortnight ago about our ghost that no one's ever seen."

Mrs. Fanning smiled and looked very wise and mysterious, and said, "Yes, dear, but don't say that no one's ever seen."

"Well, there was one part of it I quite forgot to tell you," went on Felicity, with her engaging air of childlike innocence.

"What was that, dear?" said Mrs. Fanning.

"It's only supposed to appear one fortnight every fifty years. And——" Felicity looked surprised, as if she'd made a sudden discovery, "why—it's this fortnight, this last fortnight it's supposed to have come. What nonsense it all is! No one's even seen it!"

Mrs. Fanning looked yet more wise and mysterious.

"Don't say that, my dear child. Perhaps the most psychic member of this party *has* seen it. Perhaps it has brought some message to the most psychic member of the party that—er—that the most psychic member of the party perhaps can't *quite* understand, but is grateful for the experience. Of course, no one really psychic *talks* about these experiences." She looked thoughtful for a minute, then said, "Then it won't appear again for fifty years, then?"

"No," said Felicity, "not according to the legend."

Mrs. Fanning did a hasty mental sum in arithmetic.

167

"I may be rather old by then," she admitted, "but if I can I'll try to come back to Bridgeways Hall for the second part of the message. I am sure that I have so far had only the first. The second will make it intelligible. In any case I feel that I have been greatly privileged, and it is an experience I shall never forget."

Felicity went to bed and had the best night she'd had for two weeks. In the morning she watched Mrs. Fanning anxiously. Mrs. Fanning was restless. She didn't seem quite to know what to do and where to go. She'd had no psychic vision in the night to tell her what to do or where to go. It was raining. She wandered about aimlessly for some time. Then she seemed to come to a sudden decision. She put on her mackintosh and went for a long walk. In the afternoon she did the same. A great relief came over Felicity. She had not sacrificed her nights' rest for a fortnight in vain.

The next day after breakfast the party split up as usual.

Mr. Partridge was just setting off for his lonely walk when his sister came up to him.

"Are you going for a walk, James?" she said.

"Yes," said James.

"I will accompany you, if I may," said his sister firmly. "I have lately formed the habit of a daily walk and think that I should find it most deleterious to my health to forgo it. In fact, I should much dislike to forgo it. If you will allow me, I will accompany you regularly on your walks."

Mr. Partridge's face lit up.

"I shall be delighted," he said.

Sheila and Felicity watched them set off in silence.

"My dear!" gasped Sheila in amazement, "it's an absolute miracle. Who and what's wrought it?"

Felicity slowly closed one speedwell-blue eye.

Chapter Eleven

Mrs. Franklin's Maid

"How's your mother, Frankie?" said Felicity from her usual perch on Franklin's desk.

Franklin smiled, and there was something of gratitude in his smile. Felicity was rather nice about remembering to ask after his mother. And it wasn't just empty politeness. She did really care. Felicity had a heart large enough to include all her friends' friends and relations.

"She's splendid," he said, "as fit as fit. I've just been getting a skivvy for her."

"Was that what you went away for yesterday?"

"Yes."

"Did you get one?"

"Yes."

"A nice one?"

"I think so. She hasn't any experience, but my mother's going to train her. She's going to her to-morrow."

"Where does she live?"

"The skiv? She lives at Larcombe."

"That's where Rosemary's going to-morrow. She's going to stay at Larcombe Towers."

"Is she? It's a god-forsaken place as far as trains are concerned. I've been trying to fix up this skiv's journey to my mother, but it seems to mean changing trains about six times, although it's only ten miles from Larcombe as the crow flies."

Felicity considered, then her face suddenly shone.

"Why, of course! It's quite simple. Masters is taking Rosemary to Larcombe. Well, then, while he's there he can call for the skiv and run her over to your mother's before he comes home. It's as simple as simple."

Franklin demurred. Lady Montague was away from home and Sir Digby was having a bad day. Neither could be approached for permission.

"Pins," he said, "remember, that I'm a stranger within the gates. Honestly, I can't commandeer the family chariots to send skivs to my mother in them."

"No, but I can," said Felicity very firmly, "and I'm going to. So don't argue about it. Just write and tell her to wait till the car comes to-morrow, and if you don't I will. And I'll tell Masters to go round for her *anyway*, so you'll only cause a lot of confusion if you send her off by train."

He yielded, laughing.

"You've got a good heart, Pins. I'll confess I was just beginning to get hopelessly lost in junctions and Saturdays Only. It was an impossible journey. I don't think I'd ever have got her there. I was beginning to think that the simplest thing would be to send her up to London, though it's right out of the way, and then get her out from there. It seemed less complicated. These country lines are the very devil."

"Well, don't worry your silly old head about it any longer because it's all settled . . . and good-bye now— Sheila's here and we're going to discuss bridesmaid's dresses really seriously."

She blew him a kiss and went out. Sheila had come over that morning and was upstairs sitting on the schoolroom table surrounded by books of historical costumes. She was going to be married to Ronnie next month.

As she passed the drawing-room Felicity heard voices and looked in. Rosemary was there with Sir Bertram Parker. Sir Bertram wasn't staying at the Hall. He had just come over to see Rosemary. He was always coming over to see Rosemary when Rosemary was at the Hall.

Rosemary looked tired and unhappy. Rosemary seemed to run about from house-party to house-party, and from dance to dance, and she always looked tired and unhappy.

Her eyes softened as they met Felicity's.

"Come in, Pins, darling," she said gently. "Do you want me?"

But Felicity didn't go in. For one thing she disliked Sir Bertram. She'd stiffened as soon as her eyes rested on his slim, sleek person.

"No thanks," she said, "Sheila's here. I'm just going up to her."

Sir Bertram was a very determined suitor. He'd pursued Rosemary unremittingly for the last six months. He'd swallowed her snubs with unexampled meekness. He remembered all her tastes. He'd humoured all her whims. He was desperately in love with her. Though she had refused him several times, she'd made up her mind to marry him ultimately. He was, of course, just the sort of man she'd decided to marry ultimately—rich, of good family, good-natured, adoring. She didn't love him, but she'd made up her mind some time ago that she didn't believe in love. Felicity had been right. Someone had once hurt Rosemary rather badly and after that she'd built up defences around her so that no one should ever hurt her again. That often happens to girls, of course, but with some the hurt goes deeper than with others. With Rosemary it had gone very deep indeed. She'd decided to expect nothing of the man she married but money. Money, she had persuaded herself, made up for the lack of everything else.

She'd been quite firm in the decision, till Franklin came to the Hall. And Franklin's coming had somehow upset it. Franklin's coming had raised again a nagging doubt, a nagging unhappiness in her heart . . . And she hated Franklin for raising the doubt in her heart. She refused even to look at what lay under her hatred of him. She wasn't going to go through it all again. She'd had enough of it. So she clung to her hatred of him. She proved it to herself again and again by her deliberate rudeness to him.

"I didn't expect you this afternoon," she said to Sir Bertram.

"I didn't mean to come," said Sir Bertram, "but I couldn't keep away."

He spoke in a maudlin sentimental voice that irritated her. She frowned. "I suppose I should feel complimented," she said with her slight drawl.

She heard the sound of the opening of the library door and then the sound of Franklin's voice and Felicity's. Her brows contracted quickly as if with pain or annoyance. Her lips tightened.

"Rosemary," pleaded Sir Bertram, "say you'll marry me. I'll make you a good husband. I'll settle six thousand a year on you. I know I've lived rather a gay life I suppose people have told you that—but —but—I'll settle down and make you a good husband.

She turned her pale face to him. It was a beautiful expressionless mask.

"I've told you I don't love you," she said.

"Yes, but—you don't love anyone else, do you?"

"No."

She said it breathlessly and as if more to herself than him.

"No, of *course* not."

"Then—say 'yes,' Rosemary."

She suddenly let down her defences. She might as well say "yes," and get it over. If it wasn't he it would be someone else. He'd got money, and money made up for other things. The "yes" had been on her lips when Felicity burst in.

Something about Felicity's radiant freshness touched her, as it often did.

"Come in Pins, darling," she said kindly. "Do you want me?"

But Felicity's face hardened into hostility when she saw Sir Bertram. The child didn't like him, of course, thought Rosemary wearily. Well, it didn't matter . . . she probably wouldn't like any man whom she—Rosemary—considered suitable.

"No, thanks," said Felicity, "Sheila's here, I'm just going up to her," and went out abruptly.

Sir Bertram had waited impatiently during the interruption. Now he turned to Rosemary again and said eagerly:

"Say 'yes,' Rosemary."

She'd just been going to say "yes," of course, before Felicity came in, but somehow she couldn't now. The memory of Felicity's face somehow wouldn't let her. She felt impatient with herself, but—there it was. She couldn't accept him here in this house—this house that held both Felicity and Franklin.

172

"You're going to Larcombe Towers to-morrow, aren't you?" she said.

"Yes."

"I'm going too. Ask me there."

"And may I hope?"

"There's nothing to prevent your hoping, of course," she said, "one may always hope."

He read a promise in her voice.

He went away well satisfied.

It was the next day.

The car stood at the door.

Rosemary, looking very tall and beautiful in her dark furs, went into the library.

Franklin was writing at the table.

"Where's my grandfather?" said Rosemary.

She spoke curtly.

A strained set look had come over his face at her entrance.

"I don't think he's downstairs yet," he said.

She received the information without even troubling to look at him, and was turning on her heel to go when he said, uncertainly, "Oh, Miss Harborough——"

She turned back again and looked at him, her delicate brows raised.

He'd felt slightly uncomfortable about Felicity's solution of the problem of his mother's maid. Rosemary certainly ought to have been consulted. . . . He stumbled on. He always stumbled when he spoke to Rosemary.

"Did Felicity tell you? . . . My mother has engaged a maid who lives at Larcombe——"

She cut him short with her most insolent drawl.

"I'm afraid I'm not interested in your mother's domestic arrangements, Mr. Franklin."

Then something happened. The set look left his face. His eyes blazed.

She looked at him, then closed the door.

"You look as if you'd rather like to tell me exactly what you think of me," she said quietly.

"I should," he said in a voice as quiet as hers. "I think that you behave like a spoilt, ill-bred child. I think that you break the most ordinary and elementary rules of breeding in treating your grandfather's employee as you have consistently treated me ever since I came here. I think that you're going to marry Sir Bertram Parker for no other reason than that he's got what you consider a satisfactory bank balance. That's no business of mine, of course. You're one of those women who are born parasites. You've never done an honest day's work in your life and nothing on earth would ever induce you to do one——"

He stopped. He was amazed at what he'd heard saying. He could hardly believe his ears. He hadn't meant to say it. He'd had no idea that he was going to say it till the words were actually out She was leaning against the door looking at him. She had gone very white.

"Have you quite finished?" she said.

She recovered something of her poise. Drawing her fur about her, she drawled:

"You needn't on my account."

The car was at the door. Felicity was calling "Rosemary."

Without another word she went from the library.

Franklin stayed where he was, staring stonily in front of him. What a damned fool he was. What on earth had possessed him to talk like that to her? He'd have to go now, of course. Whether she told her grandfather or not he'd have to go. And in a way he didn't regret it. It would be better to go than to stay here where he was always meeting her. He wouldn't give his notice to Sir Digby by word of mouth. He was going to his mother's the next week-end. He'd write from there. That would be easier.

Of course he'd miss Felicity frightfully . . .

Rosemary sat in the car without moving, almost without breathing, staring straight in front of her till the car reached the gates of Larcombe Towers. Then she seemed to awake from a trance. She rapped on the windscreen. Masters stopped the car and came round to the door.

"Weren't you going to fetch a girl from the village after you'd left the Towers?" she said.

"Yes, miss," he said, "Miss Felicity gave me orders to."

"Go there first," she said.

He looked a little mystified, but turned back from the gates and drove into the village and stopped at a cottage on the outskirts.

Rosemary descended and knocked at the door.

An elderly woman opened it. Rosemary entered.

"Your daughter was going as maid to Mrs. Franklin?" said Rosemary.

The woman looked apologetic.

"Well, she *were*, miss," she said, "an' she's all ready to go for a week to oblige till the lady gets someone else, but," coyly, "she an' her young man fixed it up like last night, an' they're to be married as soon as possible."

"So she'd really rather not go?" said Rosemary slowly.

"Well, yes, she would," said her mother, "but we don't like placing the lady awkward—I'm not that sort. I've told her she must go for a week if the lady really wants her to——"

"Oh, no," said Rosemary still slowly and thoughtfully, "I don't think it's necessary for her to go if she doesn't want to. I think that Mrs. Franklin can easily get someone else."

"Well, it would be a convenience to her if she could," said the woman.

Rosemary went down to the waiting car.

"The girl's going by train, Masters," she said.

"I see, miss. To the Towers now, isn't it, miss?"

"No. To the station."

Masters didn't trouble much about this alteration of his arrangements because it was well known in the servants' hall that Miss Rosemary was quite incalculable. So he took her to the station and she caught the first train to town.

*

It was the next week-end.

Franklin limped slowly up the flagged path that led to his mother's cottage door. He looked tired and worried. In his mind he was composing the letter which he would write to Sir Digby, resigning his post.

He was wondering how he should break the news to his mother that he would shortly be out of work again.

He was thinking of Rosemary.

It was a pretty little cottage with casement windows and a rose-covered porch. The flagged garden path was edged with lavender and bushes of rosemary and love-in-a-mist grew by the porch. Inside it was furnished with small pieces of cottage Chippendale and Sheraton that had been saved from the wreck of his father's fortune . . .

The place had a wholesome air. It seemed to hold healing in it. It seemed to breathe peace and serenity. It wasn't only the house and garden, of course. It was his mother as well. She was very small and slender with white hair and blue eyes and a smile that had been his lodestar from babyhood. He had never seen her angry, never seen her frightened or put out—always calm and with that magical serenity about her. She came at once to open the door for him. He entered the hall and kissed her, then followed her into the little sitting-room. Old-fashioned chintz curtains hung at the windows. A mahogany table caught and held the light on its polished surface and reflected sharply the bowl of roses in its centre. The armchair was upholstered in old-fashioned chintz. There was some cottage pottery on the low mantelpiece.

He sat down rather wearily in the armchair by the fireplace. He wouldn't tell her he was going to give up his job till after tea. It would be sure to worry her, of course, though she wouldn't show it.

"The maid get here all right?" he said.

"Yes . . . Jack, she's *such* a darling."

"I'm glad. She'd had no experience, of course?"

"No, but she's so easy to teach. She works splendidly. She gets up at half-past six every morning and she doesn't mind any of the heavy work. I wanted to get a woman in for the really hard work—grates and scrubbing floors and getting the coals in, but she wouldn't let me. There's a lot of heavy work to be done in these old-fashioned cottages, you know."

"I suppose so," he said absently.

He felt relieved that the maid was turning out a success, but he wasn't really thinking about it.

He was thinking about telling her that he was going to lose his job.

He was thinking of Rosemary.

"She's the most beautiful girl I've ever seen in my life," went on his mother.

He looked up surprised.

"Do you think so? I thought her rather plain."

"You're blinder than I thought you were then, darling," she said. "She's lovely, and, of course, she's a lady."

He was still more surprised. "A lady?"

"Yes. She hasn't told me exactly why she took a post like this and I haven't asked, but I suppose she had her reasons. As a matter of fact, I've made her come in here to sit with me in the evenings just because—well, because I've got so fond of her and it'd seem so absurd for her to sit by herself in the kitchen. It's ridiculous of me, of course," she went on with a little deprecating laugh, "but I feel as if she were a sort of daughter. I've never felt like this with any of the other ones, but, of course, she's obviously not of the servant class."

He looked amused.

"It's an ideal arrangement, of course," he said. "I've always wanted you to have someone like that, but from what I remember of her I shouldn't have thought she was the type to appeal to you in that way at all."

She rose smiling.

"Then, as I said before, you're blinder even than I thought you. . . . I'll go up and unpack your bag now. I know you'll just jumble anything into a drawer together if I don't. Tea will be ready in a few minutes. I told her to bring it in as soon as you came."

She went out and Franklin took up the paper from a table near and began to read it. The door opened and a girl, wearing a white apron over a black alpaca dress, entered and began to set the table. He did not look up till she had been in the room for a few minutes. Then, remembering what his mother had said about her, he threw her a quick, curious glance.

The paper fell from his hand. His eyes dilated. Every drop of blood left his face. It was Rosemary.

But there was a subtle change in her. She looked bright-eyed and happy. Her air of weary boredom, of arrogant hauteur, was gone. There was something of Felicity in her smile.

"You were wrong," she said. "I've put in seven honest days' work and they've been the happiest days of my life."

He limped across the room to her. Then to his own great amazement he took her in his arms and kissed her.

Chapter Twelve

L'envoi

They were all in Marcia's house in Westminster. Ronnie and Sheila were married and Franklin and Rosemary were going to be married next month. Rosemary had seemed quite different since her engagement to Franklin. It was as if the defences of arrogance and listlessness had crumbled away because she didn't need them any more, and what Felicity called the "nice hidden self" had come out. Rosemary had told Franklin that he needn't be conceited and think that it was all him because it wasn't—it was partly his mother. She said she'd felt quite different when she'd been at the little cottage even one day. Something of its peace had entered her soul and stayed there.

She'd admitted to herself after that first day that she loved Franklin and she realised with something of surprise that she wasn't afraid of poverty, that she'd welcome it with him. But, as a matter of fact, they weren't going to be very poor because Matthew had got a post for him as secretary to a friend of his who was in the Cabinet, and they had found a little house in Westminster not far from Marcia's.

Felicity was "coming out." Marcia was going to present her that evening, and next week Marcia and Matthew were going to give a dance for her. Much to everyone's relief, Lady Montague had said that she was too old for that sort of thing and that Marcia must manage Felicity's debut entirely. There had been one horrid moment when John and Violet had offered to do it, but Marcia had managed to put them off quite politely.

Matthew stood rather nervously by the front door in his overcoat.

"They ought to hurry," he said to Franklin and Rosemary, "it's time we were starting."

Then Felicity came downstairs, followed by Marcia. Only somehow it didn't look like Felicity. The red-gold plait was gone. Her hair was closely shingled. A feather head-dress was attached to it by a silver band. White gossamer draperies . . . pearls . . . a long train.

Franklin and Rosemary, standing side by side in the hall, both felt a sudden catch at their hearts as they thought of Felicity with her swinging red-gold plait, her schoolgirl hat and coat. That Felicity had gone for ever . . .

"Hurry up, my child," said Matthew anxiously.

"Doesn't she look sweet?" called Marcia.

"Adorable," said Rosemary sadly, "but somehow——"

"But somehow it isn't Felicity," supplied Franklin.

Felicity had let Matthew wrap her cloak around her. She was just going out of the door to the waiting motor.

She turned to them at the words and flung them a grimace.

It wasn't quite the Face, but it had a lot of the Face in it.

"It's all right," said Franklin, relieved, "it *is* Felicity."

"Yes, I don't think we need worry," said Rosemary, "it will always be Felicity."